1976

may be kept

BLINDFOLD

BLINDFOLD

by Lucille Fletcher

RANDOM HOUSE   New York

BLINDFOLD

ONE

From the very beginning Dr. Richard Fenton found the project highly questionable, but he agreed, signed the necessary papers, and on Wednesday, October 15, proceeded to obey instructions.

At six o'clock that evening, having casually told his secretary and answering service that he would be unavailable till morning (information which he felt sure would be interpreted lasciviously), he left his office at 57th and Park and headed crosstown toward Fifth. Ordinarily, at this hour he took a cab to his home on 92nd Street, or walked if he had the time. Tonight, however, the route and purpose were not ordinary.

WALK WEST THREE BLOCKS, THEN SOUTH (OR NORTH) TWO BLOCKS. HAIL A TAXI.

The air was balmy. Daylight lingered on, giving the city a golden haze. Down at the end of 57th Street hung a dazzling cloud formation, lit by the falling sun. A beautiful Indian-summer evening. Dr. Fenton moved with the rush-hour crowds, feeling himself already a disembodied man and rather liking the sensation. He had been skeptical till now, but with the adventure close at hand he was keyed up. It was a situation fit for Sherlock Holmes.

The doctor was a tall, rangy man in his early forties. He wore a tan tweed topcoat and dark brown hat, and under his arm he carried a small parcel. Rapidly covering the three blocks with long, swinging strides, he turned north at Sixth Avenue, walked up to 59th Street and hailed a cab.

Following instructions to the letter, he waited until he had slammed the door before giving his destination. Then he said, "La Guardia, please. Make it the Triboro."

In the Sherlock Holmes tradition, perhaps they should have called for him in a long sleek black car that touched the curb a second and lurched away. But the General had chosen differently.

TAKE CAB TO LA GUARDIA AIRPORT. WALK TO
AREA D. OPERATOR 10 WILL MEET YOU THERE.

Not, God knows, that there was anything so secret about La Guardia Airport. The doctor was a noted psychiatrist and the writer of a well-received book on the nature of genius. He was also a native New Yorker and a man of many friends. As such he might very well expect to run into somebody who knew him. Under the circumstances, La Guardia seemed about as clandestine a meeting place as, say, Times Square at high noon.

Passing through the terminal building and again on his way past the ticket counters, he found himself glancing covertly left and right. But he saw no one. He went unhailed.

Operator 10 was standing near a line of telephone booths, reading a newspaper. His name was Joseph Stevens and he had the sine qua non of a Secret Service man, the capacity to look unobtrusive in a crowd. As Dr. Fenton approached, he gave no sign of recognition, did not even look up.

Dr. Fentón cleared his throat, moving closer.

Stevens continued to read. He remained thus for several minutes longer, apparently engrossed in the sports page; then, carefully folding the paper, he slid it into his coat pocket, picked up the attaché case at his feet, advanced to a ticket counter, studied the bulletin board, moved to a vending machine, extracted a Baby Ruth, and finally strolled toward an unattended passenger gate. Passing through, he showed even now as little concern for the hovering Dr. Fenton as he might for a stray cat.

4

But nearing the end of the long passenger shed, he began to walk more rapidly, and just before exiting to the field he looked back and nodded. Step on it, the nod seemed to say, and don't attract attention.

With Stevens now setting a very brisk pace, and the doctor following at a distance of twenty feet or so, they threaded their way among giant planes, fuel and baggage trucks to the outermost reaches of the field. Just short of the lagoon stood a small, black, unmarked plane. Although neither pilot nor mechanic was in evidence, the plane was already warmed up, its twin engines roaring, propellers flashing.

Motioning Dr. Fenton to wait, Stevens stepped aboard.

The doctor turned, looking out over the vast reaches of the field, then at the sky. The sun had set. A few bright streaks still lingered in the west, but already rising over Flushing was a huge harvest moon. At the perfect full, it hung benignly just above the rooftops, a great golden eye.

Stevens appeared at the doorway, motioning the doctor to come aboard.

YOU WILL BE FLOWN IN A SEALED PLANE TO
A SECRET DESTINATION.

The windows of the cabin were opaque, painted over with thick black enamel. But the interior was quite handsome, quite plush. He had anticipated bucket seats, but this was no military plane. Its seats were covered with pale green linen, a carpet to match ran down the middle aisle. Save for the windows, which doubtless had been painted just for him, it looked like something that might have been custom-built for a millionaire.

As it taxied, and again as it raced down the runway and climbed up over Queens, he found himself looking automatically for the outside world, for lights, for the flash of propellers, for tilting terrain. But only the black windows stared back, and it was as though he were imprisoned in a flying clothes-closet.

The "no smoking" and then the "fasten seat belts" signs went off. Stevens flipped aside his seat belt and settled back with a grunt.

"Make yourself comfortable," he said, and these were his first words of the evening.

"It's certainly a nice little plane," the doctor said. "Does this belong to the army, or is that something I'm not supposed to ask?"

Stevens smiled. "Would you like some coffee now or later, Doctor?"

Dr. Fenton smiled in return. Even here, Stevens obviously would stay in his shell. He was the butler in this play, not lord of the manor, and he had no intention of stepping out of character.

Giving up on sociability, Dr. Fenton lit a cigarette and mused on the swiftness and unexpectedness of the events that had carried him to a blacked-out plane, with a man named Stevens, flying above the clouds toward a shadowland.

Three days ago he had been moving placidly through the routine of life. Then, in quick succession, had come the initial telephone call, the meeting with the General in the hotel room, the appeal to patriotism, and, let it be confessed, the challenge. "You may very well be our final hope," the General had said. The doctor had signed his name, taken solemn oaths.

Stevens, having finally exhausted the pleasures of the sports page, was now frowning over a crossword puzzle while he munched on a Baby Ruth candy bar. The doctor glanced at his watch. It was seven-thirty. He had not been told how long the flight would take, only that he could count on being back at La Guardia by two in the morning. Under the circumstances it might be a good idea to get some sleep. He tilted the seat back and tried, but sleep did not come.

Idly he watched Stevens for a while, then asked, "Will it be a breach of anything if I stretch my legs a little?"

Stevens looked up solemnly. "Go ahead. You've got the run of the plane. Say, do you happen to know a three-letter word for desire?"

The doctor stood in the aisle, yawning. "Yeh?"

"Good," said Stevens.

The doctor moved up the aisle, past the empty seats, once again acutely aware of the loss of bearings, the loss of any sense of direction. North? South? West? He could not even guess. The door to the cockpit was closed, and it came as a surprise to think that beyond it was a human being. Long since, he had given himself over to the feeling that he and Stevens were alone on this plane, and that an automatic pilot was at the stick. There was equipment for serving meals, and an electric coffee pot stood ready. The lavatory was a tiny, luxurious lounge, handsomely appointed except for the black paint that had been slopped over its window. The wastebasket was empty; there were cakes of soap in plain wrappers. He smiled. No detail had been slighted.

La Guardia, of course, would have a record of the flight. He might be able to check. But that would be churlish. The secrecy all had a point, and he had accepted the assignment under their terms. He walked back to his seat and suggested to Stevens that maybe it was about time to plug in the coffee pot.

It was around eight-fifteen when the plane finally began to lose altitude. Stevens grew alert.

"May I have your blindfold, Doctor?"

The doctor handed over his parcel. "I hope it's okay," he said, smiling. "I went to four stores this morning before I found one with a blindfold department."

> YOU WILL WEAR A BLINDFOLD FOR THE FINAL
> STAGE OF YOUR TRIP, WHICH WILL BE BY
> AUTOMOBILE.

Stevens was shaking out the large square of black silk, testing it over his own eyes for density and translucence, then folding it into shape.

"Now, Doctor . . ." Stevens bound it firmly about the doctor's eyes, knotted it securely. The plane was dipping in for the landing. "Now if you'll stand here in the aisle, sir, I'll help you on with your coat."

And next the hat, jammed down over his temples. The effect must be grotesque, the doctor thought. He sat down again, blinder now than the windows, double-sealed from the world.

"Can you fasten your seat belt, Doctor?"

It was a little late for that. The wheels were hitting the landing strip, but he obeyed. The silk of the blindfold was new and it itched. His eyelids smarted. What the hell, he thought, abruptly irritated. He was forty-two years old, of good New England ancestry, and a man to whom the world had given respect and trust, and here he was, fixed up like a bank robber in a silent movie.

The plane came to a stop. His seat belt was unfastened. He heard the cabin door being opened. A hand grasped his elbow. He was in the aisle, being propelled, steered . . . The burst of fresh air at any rate was welcome.

With Stevens (at least presumably it was Stevens) still guiding him, he made his way down the steps. His feet touched soft earth, grassy and spongy. The air was warm and moist, quite different from the brisker climate he had left behind. And it had a sweet smell, a fragrance that he thought he recognized as honeysuckle.

The sounds were the sounds of deep country. Crickets and tree frogs.

"We can step right along now, Doctor," Stevens said. "Nothing in the way."

He had been thrusting his feet forward as warily as any toddler, but now, urged along by the firm grip on his arm, he moved forward at a faster clip. Then abruptly he paused, startled by the sound that broke the stillness.

Incredibly enough it was the sound of laughter . . . or,

perhaps more precisely, the concerted chatter and hum of a cocktail party. It sounded reasonably close. At least a hundred people . . . standing about with glasses in hand . . . chattering, laughing, amused probably by the sight of a man blindfolded. Standing on the terrace of a large estate, maybe . . . It was like being discovered, naked, on the stage of the Metropolitan Opera.

It didn't take too much to make them laugh, he thought. If the sight of a blindfolded man tickled their funnybone, then they could profitably invest a few dollars in a session of analysis or two, and he personally would be glad to accommodate them.

"Here's the car, Doctor," said Stevens. "Step up about six inches, and watch your head."

TWO

They rode at high speed along a smooth-paved highway through what obviously must be open country. The car he at first judged to be an ordinary sedan, and then he realized that what he and Stevens were sharing was not the back seat at all. The car had to be a station wagon, for there was someone behind them in a third seat, someone who smoked Prince Albert tobacco and who had a wheezing cough.

Not only open country, but remote country, he surmised, for seldom did the driver cut his speed and then only for curves, never to the slower pace that would have meant a village, a traffic light, or even an unprotected crossroads. Not once did the doctor hear the sound of other cars.

The South, he felt positive. Virginia? Tennessee? North Carolina? Some area approximately two hours' flying time from New York, although this was mere conjecture. For all he knew the pilot might deliberately have taken a circuitous route. In their labyrinthine precautions nothing was impossible.

But the South, unmistakably. The warm air, the scent of honeysuckle were evidence enough. And if the South, and if lonely country, what good would it have done his curiosity even to have the blindfold removed? He knew nothing of the South, and the United States was full of dark country roads. Tonight, of course, it would not be truly dark, for the full moon was tracking above them. He pictured it riding through the clouds, silvering the road.

They were crossing a bridge. Loose planks rumbled beneath wheels. It was a surprisingly long bridge. What did it span? A good-sized river, quite obviously. The condition of the bridge seemed out of keeping with the excellence of the highway. The observation was bemusing but far from enlightening.

The car was slowing now, but not coming to a stop, merely making a sharp right turn. Stevens' shoulder nudged him. "Oops," said Stevens. "Sorry."

"It's all right," the doctor murmured. "Are we almost there?" Being deprived of sight supposedly sharpened the other senses, but it certainly did nothing for his own sense of time. It was almost eight-thirty when the plane landed. He could not guess the time now.

"Not far," said Stevens.

With the right turn they had entered a road that could not even be dignified by the term secondary. Their pace diminished to a crawl. The road was quite obviously of hard-packed dirt, deeply rutted. The car jolted, tilted. A branch brushed the roof. And then another, and then many more in succession, almost metronomic in effect. The army, he thought wryly, might invest in a pair of pruning shears and get to work on those trees.

They were slowing, stopping. The ignition was cut off. Stevens got out, reached across the seat for Dr. Fenton's arm and helped him down. There was a deep smell of pine. There were pine needles beneath his feet. A clearing in deep woodland, or so it seemed. Steered by Stevens, he made his way hesitantly along a trail of sorts that led soon to a surface of gravel. He felt a sharp sting just below his left ear, then heard the buzz of a mosquito.

Mosquitoes in October?

He heard the soft lapping of water. "A bridge here, Doctor," said Stevens. "It's a little uneven. Careful. It's narrow as hell."

A planked bridge, more of a narrow dock, he thought. It was like walking blind over the dock where his brother Phil kept his sailboat. A soft plank here and there. Abruptly Stevens grabbed him, steered him a little to the left. What the hell, he thought. "Base X" is what the General had called it. Blandly, quite blandly. He had envisioned being removed from a car and taken directly to a modern service hospital, not falling off a lousy rotten bridge.

They had crossed the bridge. Now they were in wet grass, wading through it. On this side, the smell of the water for some reason was much sharper. It had a dank smell, a smell of rotting fish and decaying vegetation. It was the smell of a windless night with the tide out. Inland water; swampland.

A voice called guardedly, "Who goes there?"

"Stay here a second, please, Doctor." And Stevens left him. Stevens was rustling through the tall wet grass. A night bird cried. And suddenly the feeling of exhilaration returned. Old memories stirred. He was reminded of the vacation spots of his childhood; the Adirondacks, Lake George, when he swam alone at night, or lay on his back studying the stars.

Where were the others? The driver, and the guy who smoked Prince Albert?

Stevens returned, and once more he was led forward. He heard the click of a gate latch, the murmur of voices. He was now on a brick walk. "Single file," Stevens said. "The bricks are uneven." From behind, he propelled the doctor carefully forward. The walkway was bordered with foliage. It had an aromatic smell, and when he brushed against it, he realized that it towered above him, closely bunched. It must be boxwood, ancient, enormous, and hence very valuable. What was the army doing with such boxwood?

Steps now, three wooden steps, yielding and creaking beneath his feet; then a wooden porch. Their footsteps sounded loud and hollow; and then through a door, and beneath his feet there was a rug and in his nostrils the smell of age and mold. And beyond these, the smell of coffee brewing, and the smells of floor wax and a disinfectant. The door was closed behind them. Stevens was fumbling with the blindfold.

The doctor blinked, at first unable to focus. The room was dazzlingly lit, incongruously, with four large ceiling globe lights.

"Well, here we are, Doctor," Stevens said.

His eyes slowly grew accustomed to the glare, the quick transition. He was standing in an enormous room that bore no resemblance to anything medical. It appeared to be the drawing room of a very old house. The four globe lights, he judged, had been recently installed. From the center of the ceiling hung a gorgeously ornate crystal chandelier with prisms. Above a marble fireplace hung a cracked pier glass, framed in gold. Dimly reflected in the old glass, he saw himself rubbing at his eyes. The walls were papered with ruby-colored wallpaper, etched with gilt, some Chinese design. There was gilt decoration and the ceiling was intricately ornamented. Save for the small rug at the doorway, the floor was bare, with old random-width boards.

But the room had been stripped of the furnishings that once must have lent it the grace of another century. In a corner to his left stood a leather couch and two straight chairs. There was a cuspidor and an old-fashioned standing ashtray. At the opposite end of the room was a desk. A gooseneck lamp stood on it. Next to the lamp was a microphone. Another microphone hung from the ceiling.

The windows had been boarded up from the inside.

But the most significant object in the room was the "screen," if such it might still be called. Across one wall a sheet of canvas had been nailed, almost obscuring what must once have been the graceful outline of an eighteenth-century arch.

"The staff will be right in," Stevens said. "Dr. Throckmorton, you know about him . . ."

"Yes," said Dr. Fenton.

Stevens took his topcoat and his hat and the black kerchief. "He'll take it from here," he said. "Excuse me, sir, I have to hand out the mail."

Dr. Fenton approached the canvas, then paused, looking up at it and frowning. "A screen" the General had said. He had pictured something like the sort of screen that might separate the beds in a hospital room. Certainly not this opaque monstrosity. God, he thought, it's almost the size of a mainsail. He touched it. It was taut, nailed securely into the woodwork, or perhaps a specially constructed frame.

Beyond this screen, a man.

> THE PATIENT'S IDENTITY, HIS NAME AND HIS APPEARANCE MUST REMAIN UNKNOWN TO YOU. YOU WILL SPEAK TO HIM THROUGH A SCREEN.

A door swung open.

THREE

Dr. William Throckmorton was a slim little man with thinning white hair and a diffident smile. In his hospital whites, he looked immaculate, indeed antiseptic, from head to toe.

Shaking Fenton's hand, he introduced himself in a most

self-effacing manner. He had been looking forward eagerly to this evening. He had read and enjoyed the doctor's book. Most interesting, he said, that the doctor had chosen psychiatry when his father and grandfather both had been surgeons.

He had been here at Base X about ten days, he said, taking a seat on the leather couch, motioning Dr. Fenton to do likewise. He was more or less in charge—"of the patient's health, that is." A Major Edward Brown was responsible for Security, all under the General's command, naturally. Living at Base X as well were five other men, two sentries, two orderlies and a cook. Would, incidentally, Dr. Fenton like some coffee? The cook had just made a fresh pot. Perhaps later, then.

Dr. Throckmorton knew little of psychiatry. Surgery was his field. He had retired as an army surgeon, on full colonel's pay, just fifteen years ago this month, settling in Virginia— "a nice little old town named Bridgewater"—and then two weeks ago the General had telephoned.

"They had to have some sort of medic here. And the reason they picked me"—here Dr. Throckmorton began to chuckle—"was my entire lack of a wife. I am a bachelor. You too? Congratulations." And he laughed heartily.

He then spoke with idealism about this present mission. Although Dr. Fenton, as a civilian, must remain substantially in the dark, it was, believe him, work worthy of the sacrifice.

Under the influence of this pleasant little man, the eerie effect of the old room began to wear off. It was reassuring to hear him talk. But he was of little help so far as the patient was concerned. He was not at home with psychiatric terms. He had an old-fashioned concept of insanity. Indeed, he seemed actually awed by his sick charge.

"That fellow is a handful. He can blow up a storm. He's crazy as a June bug." Dr. Throckmorton shook his head.

"And he even wears a mask, you know. Or did you know? A damn old dirty pillowslip, mind you. And fights just like a tiger if anybody tries to take it off. We can't shave him. Can't

14

dress him properly. The army psychiatrist said it was *guilt*."
And here Dr. Throckmorton nodded significantly.

He referred repeatedly, if vaguely, to the army psychiatrists' reports, finally handing them over.

Dr. Fenton accepted the sheaf of papers eagerly. Two excellent men had seen the patient before and after his removal to Base X and both were most discouraging. He began to read. "Do you mind, Doctor?"

"Of course not." Dr. Throckmorton left the room quietly.

He returned presently, followed by a uniformed Negro bearing coffee, and by Major Brown, also in uniform. Brown was a red-faced, stocky individual, perhaps fifty, who asked if Dr. Fenton would like a "fill-in on the layout."

The doctor laid aside the dossier, watching as Major Brown, with evident pride, called his attention to the vast expanse of canvas. Just behind this were double doors, which moved on rollers. When closed, as they were now, they provided a soundproof wall between the drawing room and the sickroom. They were electrically operated by a push button.

The microphone on the desk would serve a triple purpose. Ordinary conversational tones were audible through the "screen," but with the microphone there to amplify the patient's voice, the doctor would be sure to hear clearly the slightest whisper. The microphone was also necessary as a means of recording all conversations on tape. Finally, it made possible a monitoring system: it would carry both voices back to a remote-control booth, where, when it was deemed the patient was discussing subjects prejudicial to Security, the amplifying system would cut off and a buzzer would be sounded to drown out his voice until the doors could be shut.

"So that's about the size of it, Doctor," Major Brown said, and draining his cup, retired from the room.

Good God, who was this patient? Diplomat? Industrial genius? Military leader?

Whoever he was, his mental health, his cure, was of utterly

mammoth importance to the United States, that much was clear.

And so a special spot had been found, a hand-picked group of dedicated men had gathered: a Negro cook, a major skilled in electronics, a retired surgeon, and the others. Here they would remain, in effect prisoners, until he, Dr. Fenton, set them free. How? By curing a shadow-man behind a screen. With a monitoring system free to interrupt; with censorship perched on his shoulder like a vulture.

He finished his coffee and told Dr. Throckmorton that when the patient was ready they could begin. The time by then was ten-fifteen.

FOUR

In the large barren room, the doctor sat at his desk and lit the gooseneck lamp.

Dr. Throckmorton returned. The patient had been awakened and told that a new doctor would talk with him. His bed had been pushed up close against the other side of the screen. He had been given a mild stimulant. He had stirred, muttered something or other. A dim light burned beside his bed, Dr. Throckmorton said. The night orderly was with him.

Dr. Fenton pressed the button. Behind the screen the doors squealed slowly open. They needed oiling badly. That was something Major Brown must remedy. The movement of their opening rippled the canvas. Little puffs of dust skidded in the draught across the floor boards. At his right hand, the microphone began to hum. It was a poor and clumsy start.

He counted ten and waited, while the noises died, till he could hear the ticking of his watch.

"Good evening," he addressed the screen.

16

There was no sound in reply, only the mechanical echo of his own voice, too loud and too self-conscious. He must keep it casual, key it lower.

"Good evening. How do you do? My name is Richard Fenton."

No reply. He expected none. Picturing the trapped man, wild-eyed, just roused from sleep, quite possibly bewildered by these new demands, he sought for words that might prove calming—explanations, reassurances.

He began to speak, explaining his great interest in the case, mentioning its importance to the government. He explained the screen and microphone setup and their purpose, for he felt that he must address this man intelligently. Was he not a "genius," according to the General? He spoke gently, pausing often, and asked no direct questions for a good ten minutes or more, trying hard to concentrate only on the unseen, unknown man rather than on the audience at the control center. Even so, he was aware of that tense group and aware that what he said was being taped and would be heard next day by the General. He must eliminate that awareness by a feat of concentration, but it was a nuisance to deal with microphones. He might as well be addressing his subject two thousand miles away by telephone. It was hard to believe that the patient was just beyond that expanse of canvas.

Choosing his words carefully, he tried to pierce that canvas with his voice and eyes. He tried to clothe the man beyond with flesh and blood. He knew from the reports that the man was young, a few years younger than himself, but whether he was tall or short, or dark or light, how fat, how thin, he could not hope to know. These details hadn't been supplied. There would be no photograph. He had no notion of the man's wealth or his work, little about his home life. He knew the bare facts of his family background, that he was married, had a son. Time might provide more details, but he had never worked with so few.

"Would you care to speak to me?"

The patient's previous symptoms had consisted of a cata-
tonic stupor in which he lay in stony apathy, alternating
with excitement during which he shouted and kicked his
keepers. Obviously tonight he was in no mood to rant. Nor
was he tempted in any way by a persuasive voice from no-
where, a few glib come-ons.

Frankly, common sense decried the possibility of a response.
What must it be like in there, to be that man? To be hustled
off from home to this no-man's-land where strangers poked
and prodded. To see no sky for eleven days. His windows also
were boarded up, according to the reports. This entire estab-
lishment was under blackout. To that poor fellow, all that had
occurred here must seem more mad than his own madness,
Lilliputian maneuvers of the blackest dye. One more doctor
couldn't mean a thing.

He stopped talking.

Insight, ingenuity, cleverness and, perhaps above all, en-
during patience would be needed. He must not press too hard.
The apparatus had worked. He had planted who he was.
He had heard some sounds, some breathing and some rustles.

"Good night," said Dr. Fenton. "It's been a privilege to talk
with you. I will be back on Friday evening."

He pressed the button again. The doors squealed shut. The
dust flew again along the floor.

Stevens came in with the blindfold and his overcoat. He
was steered back out into the damp night air, and back once
more over the bridge.

They landed at La Guardia at five minutes of two.

FIVE

"Patient is white, male, thirty-eight years old. Illness began
on September 28 . . ."

Lying in an old plaid bathrobe with a notebook on his knee, Dr. Fenton the next evening began collating the case reports. He had not been permitted to bring back any documents, but the facts were fresh in his mind, and getting them down on paper might help.

He had seen the reports of the two army psychiatrists, statements made by persons present when the patient first became ill, a statement from the patient's personal physician, another from the orderlies, and he had talked personally of course with Dr. Throckmorton. He also had received a summary during his interview with the General. This might seem like a great deal, but it added up to very little.

Dinner was over. It was a rainy, windy evening. He had a fire going in the library fireplace and Beethoven's Pastoral Symphony, an antidote for such a night, on the hi-fi. He liked working with music in the background. It also served to insulate him against the noises of the big house. Ed Williams, a neurologist, in from the West to make a speech tomorrow night at the Waldorf, was bellowing in the shower upstairs. There was a clatter of pots and pans in the kitchen below, where Louisa, his large blond housekeeper, was indomitably making grape jelly. Lord Lister, the household parrot, sang and screeched alternately. And the telephone kept ringing, as often as not for Louisa.

Patient X. White. Male. Age, thirty-eight.

He began to write.

Disloyalty seemed the keynote of this case, but what had caused it nobody knew. The patient's breakdown had come with little warning—some headaches, a few absences from the office, undue irritability, nothing more. Then, on the afternoon of September 28, said white male threw in the sponge. He began to yell. He yelled vituperations against his work, his colleagues and the government of the United States. Then he tore important documents to bits, kicked his desk and tried to strike his secretary, who had rushed in alarm to the telephone. When he was bundled off by the MPs, he struggled, tried to escape, and then wept hysterically.

A period of contrition had then set in. During this period, in his bed at the base infirmary, he had taken the pillowslip from his pillow and pulled it down over his face. He had wept for hours, uncontrollably. But when an army psychiatrist appeared, he began to rage again. He despised the army, he said, and threatened to disclose the secrets of his work, if they did not leave him alone. He shouted so violently, so unremittingly, that it was not thought wise to keep him within earshot of the others in the infirmary. He was given a sedative and taken home.

Even here he continued to rave. His wife could not explain the cause of his behavior. She thought it was due to overwork. Despite his youth he was a "top man" and had been an excellent, dedicated servant of the United States for the past eleven years, taking little annual leave. Nobody could believe that his anger and his treason were rational. But his threats and the nature of his work, the facts he had been dealing with, made him a security risk. He persisted, and his voice penetrated even the closed windows of his house. Under the circumstances, even a military hospital was deemed unsafe. His case went to the General.

Dr. Fenton had not heard the telephone ring, but from somewhere in the distance Louisa was bawling, "It's Miss Monica on the phone . . ."

"Ask her if I can call her back," he shouted.

The patient was transferred to Base X by automobile on October 4, just twelve days ago. There another military psychiatrist had a go at him.

This man had sat two full days in close attendance. He had also done some research on the patient's personal life. His decision had been to call in a civilian and he had recommended Fenton. He felt that using a civilian might at least resolve the matter of the patient's seeming phobia against the government. For by now the patient was refusing to talk at all.

That the patient's problems were emotional, both psychiatrists and, later, a neurologist agreed. There had been a careful physical and neurological examination and an encephalogram which did not disclose any evidence of organic brain disease. No evidence of cancer or of epilepsy, or of neurological disorder. He had been a man in excellent physical health, according to his family physician. He did not drink, did not take drugs, did not even smoke. He was "high strung" but quite normal.

Socially, he seemed to have followed a pattern of extreme reserve. Dedicated to his work, he spent long hours at it, often working at night. This gave him little time for friends or hobbies. He did, however, have an interest in jazz music. He had an expensive sound system and a large collection of records. Though he might seem uninterested in them now, he was by all accounts devoted to his wife and his four-year-old son. His wife was ten years younger than her husband. The child was sickly.

"Well . . ." Ed Williams appeared at the doorway. "A case? Anything sexy?"

"Hardly," the doctor said.

"I thought it was *always* sexy," said Williams, who as a neurologist had an irreverent view of psychiatry.

"Not this one. At least I don't think so." The doctor snapped his notebook shut.

"Don't be too sure," said Williams. Leaving, he called from the hallway, "It's what pays your salary, did you ever think of it that way?"

"You should be practicing your speech instead of bar-hopping," Dr. Fenton replied. He got up, turned the record over, opened the notebook again, and then sat there, gazing into the fire. He knew Williams was baiting him, and yet . . . sex?

He started writing again.

Among the neighbors, the patient and his wife were known as quiet, reserved, shy, but always pleasant. The wife attended church, attended P.T.A. meetings, grew prize camellias, and gave an impression of contentment. No fights had marred the marriage, so far as anyone knew. No scandal had been breathed. No mistresses for him, no lovers for her, no debauchery. Successful marriage, tranquil private life. The wife could assign no cause for the breakdown, and so . . .

The doctor began doodling, listened for a few minutes to the symphony.

And so far as anyone knew, a normal childhood. He had gone to public schools (unspecified), where he had shown an early aptitude for his field, whatever it was. His parents, people of ordinary means, had contrived to send him to an excellent university, with the aid of a scholarship. He had been urged on by admiring teachers to take a graduate degree and then another. At twenty-seven, after brief stints at teaching and in private industry, he had entered government service.

A scientist? Almost certainly a scientist.

"I'm going to my room now." Louisa's arms were stained purple all the way to the elbows. She was rubbing them on an empurpled apron. "And if you're wondering what that is hanging on the kitchen faucet, it's the jelly bag. I knew you'd be asking me, so I'm telling you."

He smiled. "That's very thoughtful of you, Louisa."

She snorted. She was peeved at him, he knew, because he had not taken Monica's telephone call. Louisa had been his housekeeper for twenty years. She stood there, and something was obviously on her mind.

"You ought to get a new bathrobe," she said.

"Christmas is coming. You can give me one."

Still she stood there, looking around for something to find fault with, he judged.

"You call Miss Monica back?" she asked finally.

"Not yet."

"Hmph."

She was dying to ask him where he had been last night, he felt sure. Well, it would have to remain none of her business (Monica's either). He hated to see Louisa in such acute distress. He knew he could end her misery with a small lie; but it was bad enough to have to apologize to his secretary, Edna

22

Willoughby, and to his answering service, without fabricating a story for Louisa.

"Why don't you try some Clorox on those arms, Louisa?" he said, grinning. "You'll ruin the sheets."

"Don't you worry about the sheets," she said, and, snorting, she left.

He picked up the pencil again, opened the notebook.

Yes, almost certainly a scientist.

Or was he?

Dr. Fenton began to doodle again. He put down the notebook, made himself more comfortable. His eyes closed, and he saw the room in the old house, with its crystal chandelier and the screen.

He dozed.

He came awake with a start, with a feeling of guilt. You damned fool, he thought. If you want to sleep, go to bed.

He got up and turned off the phonograph. Innocent though it might seem, what he had just done could be interpreted as treason against the United States.

I SWEAR THAT I WILL NEVER DIVULGE THIS MATTER TO ANYONE.

With him asleep, what would prevent someone from picking up the notebook and reading it? A far-fetched thought of course, but was it any more far-fetched than the blindfold and the black windows of the plane? The General had set the rules, and he had sworn to abide by them.

Tearing the pages from the notebook, he threw them into the fire, waiting until they had burned to ash.

SIX

The rain continued for several days, and it was through a steady downpour that Dr. Fenton made his second trip. This time he did not hear the chattering voices at the landing field, but then of course people wouldn't be drinking on an outdoor terrace in the rain. And what a rain! The blindfold was soaking wet when Stevens took it off. His overcoat was drenched and his shoes soaked and muddy. Dr. Throckmorton thoughtfully provided slippers, while Stevens took his shoes out to be dried. Still chilled, he sat down finally before the screen.

The heat had been turned on. He could hear the hum of an oil burner. The old-fashioned radiators clanked. Occasionally there was a hollow clattering from above, as though a squirrel were scampering over a tin roof, or a nut had dropped from a tree.

The patient's condition had remained unchanged since Wednesday night. He had not referred to the doctor's visit, nor appeared any different for it. A drug the doctor had suggested was being given him. It had not had a perceptible effect upon his disposition.

Dr. Fenton pressed the signal button.

The doors rolled open, this time without squeaking. The microphone had no hum. Major Brown had obviously been at work. The apparatus was in excellent working order. Behind the screen there was a footstep, and then a cough, a confiding whisper. "He's here. Now try to talk. He's here to help you . . ." The cajoling tones of Dr. Throckmorton.

"Good evening. I am Richard Fenton."

Richard Fenton, ready to try again.

"I am here to help you."

Dead silence.

"How do you feel this evening?"

Not a sigh, not even a rustle from the other side of the screen.

In an ordinary case, of course, with a patient deeply uncommunicative, he could sit for hour upon hour, through session after session, saying nothing. Under ordinary circumstances he could hope to accomplish something merely by his presence in a room, by the friendliness of eyes and face. But here this was impossible. If he sat like a dummy, waiting, the patient would be offered no stimulation whatsoever.

After more questions and more pauses, awaiting answers that did not come, he began to talk. He talked about the weather, about New York, about autumn, and even about jazz music, of which he knew little. But his comments, through their very emptiness, might just possibly get a contemptuous rise from an aficionado.

Nothing.

Again he heard Dr. Throckmorton whispering. "Now you know good and well you're listening, sir. It's interesting. Now why don't you talk to the doctor? He's trying hard to help you."

Dr. Fenton smiled. "Dr. Throckmorton," he said. "No disrespect intended, but I think it might be better if you leave him to me."

"I was just trying to do a little pump-priming," Dr. Throckmorton replied. "But just as you like."

He heard sounds indicating that Dr. Throckmorton was leaving the patient's bedside. He wondered if he had been offended, but, good God, there were enough nuances to deal with already . . .

He looked at the list of subjects he had scribbled while on the plane. Eliminating the patient's work as a topic was a tremendous handicap. A man's work was a good half of his life.

"Do you miss your wife?" he asked.

25

No answer.

Was she pretty? Did she cook well? Any hobbies that they shared? He moved to the child. Did the patient play ball with his son? Did he read to him? He understood the boy was frail, was that true? No answer. No answer. No answer. He was beginning to know every ripple on that screen. The sound of his voice was becoming emptier and emptier.

An hour passed, and then another. When it became time to leave, the doctor had covered all the subjects in his notes and the key emotions of life. He had spoken humorously, he had spoken seriously, he had presented himself as a minister and a friend. Telling too much about himself for a man whose nature and job were self-effacing, he ended up feeling like a sounding brass and a tinkling cymbal. But he had failed to win even a sound, one telltale groan or sigh. The man still lay in darkness, as though dead.

Stevens came in at last, bearing the doctor's shoes. They were stiff, but warm and polished. Then there were more handshakes and some coffee, more stumbling through the rain. He was soaking wet again by the time they got to the plane.

On Monday evening, the pattern was repeated. He added a few new subjects to his list, and he touched upon the vital question:

"What do you have against the United States?"

This brought no reply, as usual. It was a warm night once again. Indian summer, after that fierce stab of winter, had returned. The red room (he had begun to call it that because of the color of the wallpaper) looked much cleaner tonight (the floor boards had been waxed), but it was stuffy with its boarded-up windows, and the radiators still shed warmth. Leaving his desk from time to time, the doctor paced. He smoked too many cigarettes, and drank cup after cup of the strong coffee which the cook had left beside the leather couch. The silences dragged.

He was beginning to feel an identification with the other

psychiatrists who had tried and failed, men who had had the sense to give this enigma up. The novelty of adventure had worn off. These night journeys had become a burden.

Putting out his cigarette, he tried again.

He began to speak of genius and its nature. Yes, that was a matter very close to both their hearts. He had been interested in the patient because he'd heard he was a genius. He himself had studied the lives of several talented men, in an attempt to analyze what made them so remarkable. Would the patient care to share his humble findings on that score?

No response, except a false one. Somebody with a deep bass voice had cleared his throat. But that was Joe, the colored orderly who was on duty now. He'd heard that voice before.

Joe was interested in psychiatry. He too had read the doctor's book. He was probably leaning forward now, alertly, in the dark, primed to catch it straight from the horse's mouth.

Genius, the doctor said, was a special gift of God. As far as he had determined, it had no link to race or parentage. Genetics could not calculate it. Beethoven's mother, for example, had been the daughter of a cook, and his father an alcoholic. Seldom was it passed on from father to son. It stood alone, a special gilt-edged sixth sense, and its possession enabled one to leap where other men must crawl. Yet—and now he spoke with penetration, slowly—it often took its toll of human strength.

It could involve much suffering . . . He paused. No sound, except the creaking of a chair. That bed in there could not creak. It was a metal hospital bed. It moved on rubber wheels.

Sometimes the problems of a genius were simply physical, he continued. The mind worked tirelessly, with a contempt for common sense. But the limited body wearied. The nerves gave out. And the strain produced—well, ordinary symptoms in some, like migraine headaches or an ulcer. He had heard that the patient suffered from upset stomachs, occasional headaches? Had they followed a period of overwork?

Silence.

What had the patient taken for those headaches? Had rest or a change of scenery helped?

No answer.

Then again, he said, such physical signs, if disregarded, could not always serve as outlet for the conflict. The ambitious mind, frustrated by the body, grew more and more overwrought. Grotesque behavior sometimes ensued, and acts were committed which were not germane to a situation. Words were flung which were not really meant. The genius might even enter a shadowy world where reality, as the world regarded it, ceased to exist. This was not shameful, nor should such acts of sheer exhaustion and frustration be taken seriously by intelligent men.

If the patient felt that he had been pressed on his job too hard, either by his own ambition or the ambition of his employers, he should say so. One act of "treason" did not beget a court-martial. Not after many years of loyalty. The patient's words would be forgiven.

Indeed, Base X itself should seem a form of hope. So were the presence of psychiatrists. This was not a prison at all, nor they his keepers. He was keeper over them. All would be done to aid his genius and restore it.

Once again he waited.

Absolute silence.

Everybody would be more than delighted to have him back, under any terms. He could go on a long vacation. He could have a period of rest at home. Anything he pleased. He could work shorter hours. Was it a matter of pay? Anything financial troubling him? The doctor doubted it, for it had been his experience of genius that money seldom was a goal. Nor even fame, one's name in lights. Genius usually worked for the love of the work alone. But if the patient disagreed with this . . . ?

Once more, no answer.

No sound.

He coughed, went on.

Genius suffered often in its social relationships. Love, family and friends could, under the strain of trying to "fit in," often seem like crushing burdens. There were so few who understood the powerful driving force of talent. One's loved ones might seem to understand, but there were bound to be periods of estrangement, when a man or a woman or one's colleagues seemed to fail, when barriers rose, and the genius stood alone.

Then hatred, bitterness could set in, unfounded perhaps on facts. But if a personal hate or a sense of loneliness existed in the patient's domestic life, Dr. Fenton would like to know of its existence. Confession would harm no one.

No one, outside this place, would ever be apprised of what went on here. The patient's wife would never know. Nor any of his family.

No answer.

Genius could not conform. The patient, by his acts, had led a life of outward morality. Perhaps he had not wanted to live that way. Perhaps he had desired things outside the pale of marriage, the acts of standard duty. Many geniuses, for instance, had been homosexuals, latent as well as open. Beethoven had been impotent, except with prostitutes. So had Brahms. Chopin and Tchaikovsky had deviated. All this to a psychiatrist was not so outlandish, and if in the patient's heart the knowledge of a shameful desire, or the past fulfillment of one, was the actual root of his depression, then it should be disclosed, not veiled with anger against an innocent substitute. For example . . .

His throat was dry. It was nearing eleven-thirty and time for Stevens to appear. But he pushed on, hoping still.

"For example, you may not really love your wife. You may be sorry that you married her. Trying to conceal that fact from her and from yourself and all the world, your actual desire may be to murder her."

29

"M—murder?" said a sudden, choked-up voice.

A voice of baritone quality, which seemed to come out of the grave. It stammered over the "m." But the word itself (and what a strange one to have chosen) was pronounced with refinement. Through the microphone came the sound of heavy breathing.

Dr. Fenton waited tensely.

Nothing else except the breathing ensued. He counted up to twenty.

"Do you want to murder your wife?"

For answer there came a laugh. It was followed by a short, curt "No."

"Do you want to murder anybody?"

No reply.

"Will you tell me what is wrong?"

A pause. Then there was a choking sound. Next it sounded as though the patient were vomiting. Hurried footsteps, and although the doctor had not pushed the button, the doors closed.

Still it was an achievement, and a pleasure to write at last on that blank pad: "The first response took place October 20. 11:25 P.M."

SEVEN

Mrs. French, a wealthy woman of fifty-nine, was concerned because she had abruptly and inexplicably lost all interest in "people." When Dr. Fenton opened his consulting-room door he found her eagerly stretched on the couch, eyes closed, already fingering the pearls which had proved such an aid to total recall during previous sessions.

Edna Willoughby, having just answered the telephone, and having told the caller that the doctor was about to begin a consultation, was now covering the mouthpiece with her hand. "He says it's urgent," she said.

Dr. Fenton backed out, closing the door gently on Mrs. French. Frowning, he picked up the phone.

"Dr. Fenton?"

"Yes?"

He did not recognize the voice at once. Stevens had a voice as neutral as his personality.

"Operator 10 calling, Doctor. May I ask if anyone else is on the line?"

"No . . . Excuse me a second, please." Resting the phone on Edna's desk, he headed for his other consulting room. "Hang up when I get it, will you, please, Edna?"

He picked up the other phone, waited for the click that meant she had complied, then said, "Okay now."

"Right," said Stevens crisply. "Doctor, I hope this doesn't inconvenience you too badly, but it's been necessary to cancel tonight's session. I'll phone tomorrow morning to let you know about the next one."

"I see," said Dr. Fenton. "Well . . ." He paused, somewhat surprised at the disappointment he felt. Slight though the accomplishment might be, he had been carrying around a sense of triumph since the patient spoke two nights before. An erratic schedule could break the continuity.

"May I ask," he said, "whether the change of plans is based on some change in the patient's condition?"

"I'm authorized to say only what I've just told you, Doctor," Stevens replied, with a faint shade of impatience.

Psychiatry was something that came in quart bottles!

Dr. Fenton drummed on the arm of the couch. "All right, it can't be helped, I suppose. Stevens, now that you've called I'd like to ask a favor. I'd planned to ask you this evening."

"What is it, sir?"

"It's a matter of vital importance that I speak with the General. Could you tell me how I may contact him by phone?"

For a few seconds Stevens was silent. "I'll see if it can be arranged, Doctor."

"If I put through a person-to-person call to the Pentagon . . ." Dr. Fenton began.

"That wouldn't work," Stevens said. "I'll see if it can be arranged, Doctor. I'll get back to you as soon as possible."

At five-thirty Mrs. French departed, assuring him that she felt the barriers would soon come crashing down. At six, Edna Willoughby left for Astoria.

When, at seven, Stevens still had not called, the doctor gave up. The evening was a waste. For this he had canceled a speaking engagement with a fee. For this . . .

"Oh, for the love of God," he said to the empty office.

He had dinner at his favorite Italian restaurant, saw a movie in which a man of fifty or so and a girl of twenty-one or so fell in love, and was home by ten o'clock.

"Is that you, Doctor?" Louisa asked superfluously, since he was already standing in the doorway. She remained, with no embarrassment whatsoever, stretched on the library couch.

"Everywhere I go I see women on couches," he said.

"I thought you were out with your new girl friend," Louisa said, making some pretense of hauling her huge frame from its place of repose.

"Don't get up, Louisa," he said. "You look much too comfortable to be disturbed." She had been reading a mystery novel he had bought himself the day before.

"You sure?" she said, settling back.

He could use the sleep.

But sleep did not come easily. He lay in the dark, addressing the man behind the screen. At times the imaginary interview was interrupted by other thoughts, these derived from the movie he had just seen. Already, he reminded himself, you're over forty. Forty-two and a half, to be precise.

At two o'clock the following afternoon Stevens called back. "Do you have a pencil, Doctor? Can you be at the Hotel Bennington at seven o'clock this evening? Room 351. Got it?"

"Yes," the doctor said. "I've got it. But what does it mean?"

"Your request is being complied with," Stevens said. "And the next session will be tomorrow night. Right?"

The doctor smiled in spite of himself. Stevens was a minor phenomenon. "Right," he said briskly, and hung up.

Did it mean that the General was coming to New York just to see him . . . just to avoid having to use the telephone? Or in Room 351 would he be catapulted into a fifth dimension where top-secret generals abided?

It meant that Monica would be sore. Although, he reflected, beginning to dial her number, sore was not exactly the word. The soreness would be only on the surface.

And what beneath? Apathy? Resignation? Or merely irritation at being inconvenienced? He really didn't know for certain, but he did know that he and Monica were acting out a charade, nothing more. She was pleasant to look at and pleasant to be with . . . and she knew he would not marry her, and she knew the reason why.

"Monica?" he said.

"Well, hello," she said.

"I have a patient waiting," he said. "I just have a second. But about tonight . . . I'm terribly sorry . . ."

Tonight they were to have been in the second-night audience of a play hailed as the best to hit Broadway in ten years.

"After what Louisa told me the other night, I wasn't counting on it," she said.

"What did Louisa tell you?"

She laughed. "That you've been staying up till all hours . . . It's all right, Dick."

"Maybe some day I can tell you about it," he said.

"Maybe I'd rather not hear about it," she said.

"You're just flattering me," he said. "Listen, I may still be able to make it. I mean, if you want to take the tickets and meet me at the theater to save time . . . But the safest thing would be for you to take the tickets and ask somebody else."

"Oh, hell," she said. "It's a lousy play. I saw the run-through." She sighed. "All right, Dick."

"It's what you get for messing around with older men," he said. "I'll send the tickets by messenger."

Since he had not been instructed to approach the Hotel Bennington by way of Lincoln, Nebraska, he took a cab direct. It was an antiquated hotel in the Chelsea district. He entered the lobby at precisely three minutes before seven, threaded his way among potted plants and took the old-fashioned open-grille elevator to the third floor.

The door was opened a crack, and he recognized the eye and bridge of the nose as belonging to Stevens. "Come in," Stevens said, graciously opening it to a full eight inches.

Dr. Fenton slipped through, and Stevens immediately slipped out, closing the door silently behind him.

"It's good to see you, Doctor."

The General, dressed in civilian clothes, was seated on a twin bed covered with a pink chenille spread, reading a Gideon Bible by the wan light of a pin-up lamp. As Dr. Fenton entered, he rose, extending his hand.

"Good evening, sir," Dr. Fenton said.

The General indicated the other twin bed, and sat down as before. His finger was inserted in the Bible. He looked at the doctor over rimless glasses. "I've just been doing a little reading," he said quietly. "Powerful stuff. I never get tired of it."

The General was a tall, broad man with waxy, almost artificial-seeming white hair. His face too was waxy, pink in hue, with a heavy nose and fleshiness about the jowls. Without the uniform, he gave the impression of a Methodist bishop.

34

"Voices crying in the wilderness," the doctor said. "Valleys being exalted . . . Tremendous."

The General smiled. He snapped the Bible shut and placed it on the night table. "Our facilities for hospitality are somewhat limited, I'm afraid." Rising, he crossed to the dresser. "I can offer you a glass of ice water, though." At the dresser he turned, lifting the pitcher.

"All right. Thanks very much."

Dr. Fenton looked about the small room. There was no luggage in sight. Not even so much as a newspaper, for that matter. The room obviously had been hired for the single purpose of this meeting, just as had been the one in early October. The topcoats spread over the chair would go; Stevens would smooth the beds, perhaps even wipe away fingerprints. Security left not a ripple.

"I'm sorry we can't offer you anything stronger," the General went on. "But of course the less attention we attract . . ." He proffered the glass of water. "I'll also ask you not to smoke, if you don't mind."

"Not at all," said the doctor.

They sipped their water. Somewhere in the lower reaches of the hotel an orchestra had begun to play. The tune was "Moonlight and Roses."

The General set his glass down on the night table.

"General," Dr. Fenton said, "I hope you didn't find it necessary to come all the way to New York just for the purpose of talking with me."

The General shook his head. "I found it necessary to be in the area," he said. "Now, sir . . ."

Dr. Fenton reached to the night table and put his glass next to the General's.

"I might say at the outset," the General intoned, "that we were all highly pleased by what happened the other night. In the light of past, shall we say, frustrations, I feel the very articulation of those few words marked a signal accomplishment."

With his fervent, measured voice, the flowing movements of his hands, he might indeed have been a man of the church.

But with these hands he had personally choked the life from six Germans during the course of World War II. His whole career had been spent in Intelligence. His only son had been killed in Korea.

"I would also like to apologize for canceling last night's session," he was saying. One side of that pink face looked as if a plastic-surgery job had been done on it. A flame-thrower?

"I understand," Dr. Fenton said.

"As I told you at our first meeting," the General said, "everything must be subordinated to Security. I realize that this can be unsettling to one's private life."

"I'm not concerned about that," the doctor replied. "My only thought was . . . well, it's a matter of continuity. Of striking while the iron is hot."

The General nodded. "Of course, of course. While we're on the subject, I'd like, if you don't mind, to offer some suggestions. I have, of course, heard the tapes. His use of the word 'murder'—the significance . . ."

"It's too early to attach significance," the doctor murmured.

"You were talking, at the time, of his wife, as I recall," the General said.

"Yes, that's right."

The General rose from the bed, paced to the dresser, then stood with his back to the window. The shades on both windows had been drawn.

"Utter silence on his part until her name came up," the General said, beginning to show excitement. "And then"—he struck his palm with his fist—"bang-o."

"It may or may not be significant," said the doctor. "Do *you* think it had significance?"

"In what way?" said the General, looking bland once more and sitting down on the bed.

"Something personally wrong in the marriage, which I have

not yet been told about," the doctor said, fixing his eyes directly upon the General's. "I'd been told that it was a good marriage."

"Oh, it was, it was, from all accounts." The General's eyes roved toward the ceiling. "Nothing certainly in the way of a scandal, Doctor. No infidelity on either side."

"Then why were you impressed?"

The General shrugged.

"As a matter of fact," Dr. Fenton went on, and now he reached automatically for a cigarette, then, remembering, put the pack away. "The lady has been on my mind for several days. And she is one of the reasons why I wanted to see you. It would help tremendously if I could talk to her. Would that be possible?"

The General cleared his throat. "I'm sorry, Fenton. No."

Dr. Fenton studied his hands. He placed his thumbs side by side, then locked his fingers together.

The orchestra below had ended "Moonlight and Roses" with a flourish. The room was silent, save for the General's heavy breathing.

"I was sure that you would eventually ask me that," the General said. "But believe me when I say that we are giving you all the latitude possible. To you, I am sure, it must seem like no latitude whatsoever. To us"—he spread his hands—" it's almost a carte blanche."

The doctor smiled.

"Some carte blanche, eh?" the General said. "I know what you're thinking, Doctor. I know what you're thinking. But you must believe me. This is a matter of—well, it's trite to call it life or death. But it amounts to that on a very, very grand scale."

"In other words," the doctor said, "for me to see the wife would amount to learning his identity?"

"That's part of it," the General said. "But only part of it. There are other difficulties." He picked up the Bible, fluttered its pages. "The wife is no longer at the installation . . . at the patient's home, *her* home, that is."

"Why did she leave?"

"She was given permission to take the child and go to another domicile while her husband is being treated. Her mother is quite ill."

"Then she is no longer under Security regulations?"

"She is—but in a looser sense. I'd prefer not to elaborate, Doctor . . ." The General looked disturbed. He shifted uneasily on the pink spread, rumpling it. "She is a very pretty woman, Doctor."

"I am immune to wives of patients, General," the doctor said, smiling.

"No, no. It isn't that. I'm not imputing a single flaw in her character. She has been staunch, co-operative . . . But, while we're on the subject, she *is* a woman with a strange attractiveness for men. They run after her, do crazy things for her. Not that she makes overtures . . ."

"Interesting," the doctor murmured. "What sort of crazy things?"

"Kid stuff." The General grunted. "*So* far. But two years ago, at the installation, it was discovered that some of the men were using photographs of her as pinups. And three months later, some fool of a marine lieutenant made an ass of himself by writing her love letters. He actually had the nerve to ask her to leave her husband and run away with him."

"Did her husband know about this?"

"Yes. And he raised Cain. He had the pinups ripped off the walls, and the lieutenant was shipped to Guam and nearly lost his commission. You see, Doctor, what I mean by the problems that might be created. Some unsavory character might fall in love with her, or *be* in love with her out of the past . . . Well . . ." His mouth twitched with finality. "Do what I say, and any information you need from her we'll get."

"It would still help," the doctor persisted—and then he changed his mind. "Then that's why you thought the patient's use of the word 'murder' had significance. Something to do with jealousy?"

The General grinned. "Doctor, that's all *your* province," he said blandly. "You're doing the analysis. I'm only here to keep you out of trouble." He rose now, Bible in hand, and his face looked grim again. "There's more to it than you'd ever dream. The patient himself, his family—you, everybody connected with this business—have to be protected. And protect you we will. If the time comes when we feel you are in peril, we will take you off the case."

The doorknob turned. Wheeling, the General faced it. It was Stevens. He slipped inside, pointed to his wrist watch.

"Yes, I know," the General said.

Stevens slipped out again.

"I'm sorry," Dr. Fenton said.

"No hurry," the General said. "They can hold the plane if necessary." He sat down on the bed again. "You do understand my feelings now about the wife?"

The doctor nodded. "If you have another second, there's another question . . ."

"Go right ahead," said the General, laying the Bible gently on the night table.

"This may seem irrelevant. It may seem as perilous as meeting the wife. But it would mean a lot to me. Can you tell me the sort of work our man is engaged in? Can you tell me *what* he is? I can make certain deductions, of course. I can guess, and perhaps I can come fairly close to a correct answer. But I'd prefer not to guess."

The General's foot began to tap on the drab rug.

"I'm not asking for his name," the doctor said. "That's of no importance. But something about his occupation, the way he spent his days . . . that's important. It could be vastly important. Particularly when we are dealing with a genius. What it will provide is a frame of reference . . ."

"A frame of reference?" The General looked up.

"Here is a man in a state of deep shock," said the doctor. "In panic . . . talking about murder . . ."

The General picked up the Bible again, rested it on his knee. Then, decisively, he put it down on the table. He rose, picked up his coat from the chair and put it on.

"This could be very ill-advised," he said. "The patient as an individual has been unpublicized. But his existence, the nature of his work, the nature of his genius are well known on a level that has nothing to do with newspapers . . . I am saying it poorly . . . but if it were known that you were caring for him, you could be . . ."

The General stood with his hands at his sides, military in bearing now, in spite of the tweed topcoat. "A ruthless race is on, Doctor. Ruthless men are competing."

Dr. Fenton rose. "I judge he is an atomic scientist."

The General looked him in the eye. It seemed a long time before he spoke. "He is a genius of the highest order," he said. "You are correct. An atomic scientist is what he is. But that does not tell the entire story. To the nation he is an anonymity. The nation may *never* hear about him—except through his works." The General clapped a hand on Dr. Fenton's shoulder. "I believe that if he can be cured, Doctor, we may yet win the race. It's not often that a man is given the chance you have been given to serve his country."

"The race?" Dr. Fenton said. "What race?"

"Let's call it the race into space," the General said. "Let's call it control of space."

"You mean the moon, and so forth?" the doctor asked.

"Exactly," the General said. "The moon, and *so forth*." He held out his hand and the doctor clasped it. "Now, if you will, Doctor, leave ahead of Stevens and myself. Stevens . . ." he called softly.

The door swung open. Stevens stepped inside. "La Guardia tomorrow evening, Doctor."

Dr. Fenton nodded. "Good night, gentlemen," he said.

When he got home, Louisa called from the kitchen that a special-delivery letter had come for him about an hour before. It was on his desk in the library.

EIGHT

Buffeted by strong winds right from the take-off, the little plane was a good twenty minutes reaching its cruising altitude. The going finally became smoother, the seat-belt sign went off, and Stevens, losing no time, moved immediately up the aisle toward the electric coffee pot.

Dr. Fenton removed the letter from the inner pocket of his jacket and examined it for perhaps the tenth time since its arrival the night before. It was in a long, plain white envelope with a smudged postmark. The address was complete, even to the proper zone number. The message was on a single sheet of lined paper, torn from a spiral notebook:

> If wish information certain scientist call Green by midnight tonight Plaza 6-2438.

No signature.

The letters had been cut out and pasted in neat rows. Silver block letters of the type used for decorating Christmas packages. A very neat job, except that the "c" in "call" had come unstuck and lay in the fold of the letter.

"Doctor . . ."

Stevens was offering him his coffee.

"Thanks very much." He drained his paper cup and waited until Stevens had done likewise. He was about to hand the letter across the aisle when Stevens said, "Doctor, how much do you charge, if you don't mind my asking?"

41

"You mean my patients? Twenty-five dollars a session, in most instances."

"Wow!" said Stevens.

The doctor smiled.

"That's good money," said Stevens. "Damn good money."

Fenton had the feeling that Stevens was interested in pursuing the subject, but didn't quite know what approach to take. When Stevens finally turned to his crossword puzzle, taking from his pocket the inevitable candy bar, the doctor held out the envelope. "This thing came special delivery last night. I thought I'd better turn it in."

Stevens accepted the envelope and examined it impassively, turning it over to look at the back, and then the front again. Finally he drew out the letter, read it, looked at the back, refolded it and slipped it into the envelope. "Hmm," he said and shoved it into his pocket.

"It goes without saying that I didn't call Mr. Green, whoever he is."

Stevens nodded. "That's right," he said.

"I don't get it," the doctor said. "How did this fellow get my name? I've only been on this thing a week."

Stevens mumbled something about somebody being very clever.

"Too damned clever, if you ask me," the doctor said.

"It doesn't speak too well for the Security system, and that's a fact," Stevens said, still not visibly perturbed.

"Do you think he's an agent?" Dr. Fenton asked. "If so, it seems a hell of an approach. He certainly has a low opinion of my intelligence."

Stevens shrugged.

"I thought these birds worked in the dark," the doctor said. "But here he is, giving me a name and telephone number— Open Sesame."

"Open Sesame?"

"I could have traced the address in five minutes. Should I have . . . ?"

"Unh-hunh." Stevens studied the ceiling of the plane for a split second. "We'll take care of it." He patted his pocket. "I'll turn this over to the General. I know he'll be glad you turned it in." He took the pencil from behind his ear. "Thanks."

It seemed incredible, and his feeling of disbelief grew even sharper as they went through the by now familiar routine of blindfold, the walk to the car, the ride, the sentry . . . Such an isolated spot, such elaborate trappings of secrecy, and yet, somewhere, somehow a spotlight might be on them. Still, he must also believe in the General's sure touch. And the letter was in Stevens' pocket.

Base X was as usual, except that Dr. Throckmorton was, if anything, more verbose tonight. He lingered a good half-hour on the leather couch. The patient had been intermittently nauseated since the breakthrough Monday evening. Monday night he had been very restless, "muttering to himself and calling different names."

"Whose?"

"Some woman's name, very often. It was as though she were standing right beside his bed. He thought one time that Joe was she—"

"What did he say?"

"Most of it we couldn't understand. Just the name. He said it over and over again. You know, he has a very bad speech difficulty—stammers a lot. It's hard for him to get the words out. He didn't used to have it."

"What did you understand?"

"I think he's worried about this woman. He kept saying something that sounded like 'Take care of yourself.' Then once, I believe, he asked her to forgive him. But most of it"— a gleam came into his eyes—"was lovey-dovey. He kept telling her how pretty she was, and so forth."

"How is he now?"

"Still very restless. Though it comes in spells. He has eaten a little better since you were here. But he won't let us feed him yet." Dr. Throckmorton sighed, picking up the coffee pot. "That mask, Doctor! It's a mess. If you could get that off, it would really help us very much. Another cup?"

"No, thank you. One's enough."

If the patient had been "restless," he seemed to have calmed down now. If he had come alive since Monday evening, he was wary. That was the trouble with being restricted to a particular evening and six hours out of a week. Patients did not perform on schedule. So, sitting with his notes before him after a disappointing silence, Dr. Fenton scribbled down a new request.

Since the microphones and recording apparatus were always here, couldn't they make some tapes during the day hours for him? Then, little would be lost, and if the patient proved quiescent during the interview period, he could spend the time listening to the previous evidence. It might prove helpful. He would transmit the idea through Stevens.

But at 9:00 P.M. some muttering began.

Dr. Fenton stopped his routine questions and listened carefully.

No names tonight. It was at first all quite indistinguishable, scarcely to be regarded as words, more animal sounds, much tossing in the bed. When words, or something like language emerged, they were pronounced in garbled fashion. And in the effort to force them out, the patient choked and gagged. But the doctor caught what he could.

Going over his entries, when the session was finally through, he had the following:

9:15. Incoherent mumbling. Something like "Wichita Falls" repeated several times. Or maybe "wish for . . ."

9:15—9:30. Moaned. Wichita Falls. Or could it be a woman's name? Wish for . . . Doesn't say. "Wish for what?" I asked just now. He stopped, lay still.

9:30—9:45. No sound.

His voice, a definite baritone. Fine quality. Midwestern accent. Breathing heavy. Big man?

9:50. Clear, rapid sentence, after gagging effort to speak. Couldn't catch all words, too fast. Asked him repeat. He isn't aware. Didn't.

10:00. Same rapid sentence. Delivery terrified and angry, as though pursued. Definite paranoia. Caught two words. "Rather." "Murder."

10:15. Has now for past ten minutes been under hallucination. Still talking angrily, rapidly. Caught words "Moon. Order of universe. Petty." Think also "Metaphysics."

10:17. Doors almost closed, and buzzer drowned out much. Wichita Falls again. Could Wichita Falls be location of home base?

10:30. He's given up. Silence for past eight minutes. No reply to any prompting.

10:35. I brought up wife and marriage. Dead end.

10:50. Still questioning him on personal relationships. Mother? Father? Silence.

11:00. Offered genius theme. No soap.

11:15. Muttering now. Again that peculiar pronunciation of Wichita Falls. He does it like wind-imitation, all one syllable.

11:20. Rapid-fire sentence, same. Word "Stars" now also came through. "Murder. Rather. Moon. Murder." Signal buzzed. Doors inched. Brown stuck head in and retired.

11:25. Silence.

11:30. Tiring. Throckmorton entered. Said he'd gone to sleep.

He took his glasses off. He sat there deep in thought, so deep in thought he scarcely listened to what Dr. Throckmorton had to say, or noted Stevens' entrance into the room. For at least he felt at closer grips with the man. This muttered testimony, direct from the subconscious, was the kind of world he knew, and priceless stuff, even though it was veiled by a

45

screen and captured by a microphone. The human mind was still the greatest mystery in this whole adventure, and the clouds before it were slowly beginning to clear.

"Doctor—"

"Yes?"

"It's ten to twelve."

"Certainly."

How minor seemed the blindfold, and how short the journey now. Even Stevens' final words fell on disinterested ears.

"I called the General about the letter."

"Hmm?"

"He said you were to disregard it, but to watch your step. Report anything out of the ordinary."

"Of course."

"Don't talk to anybody. If somebody calls you up, act like you didn't know what they were talking about. Keep clear of strangers. Don't lay yourself open, get into corners, you know the kind of thing he means."

"Okay."

Stevens unfastened his seat belt, for the plane had landed at La Guardia. "We won't be using this airport again after tonight. Monday next, we'll leave from Newark. Here are some new instructions. Please memorize them, then burn them, and—just trust the General . . ."

He said good night and stepped at last into the cab. A period of uneasiness lay ahead, more rigmarole and an even deeper vigilance. But as he sat back, these faded, and in his ears once more he heard that muttering voice. "Wichita Falls . . . Wish for . . . Stars . . . Murder . . ." Really, quite a successful evening after all. He was whistling softly as—having left the cab on 86th Street as per the plan, and walked from Lexington toward the park and 92nd—he finally entered his silent house.

On the hall table under the lamp lay another special delivery. This one was postmarked "Annandale." He was to call Mr. Green for information about a certain scientist, long distance, Jefferson 7-0603, Annandale, Virginia, collect.

NINE

The change-over to another airport did not make much difference. He merely crisscrossed through a different set of streets and took a cab to Newark. The cab fare was much higher, but it was the government's money. The plane was the same. It was growing darker earlier these nights. Daylight-saving time ended after the Friday session, and on Monday evening he left his office long after the sun had left the sky.

Green, after that initial double play, sent no more letters. on Monday Dr. Fenton turned the Annandale letter in. Stevens thanked him in the same noncommittal manner, and once more told him to keep strangers out of his life, to act like a shadow, to stay mum.

Unfortunately, the patient during the next full sessions did the same.

He seemed to have returned to apathy. The "restless" period had passed. Limp as a dead cod, he lay during these frustrating times, turning an indifferent ear to all the doctor's attempts. And during the day the microphones caught nothing. After Monday night the General agreed to the doctor's request for daytime tape recordings. But all day Tuesday the apparatus picked up little more interesting than the movements of the orderlies around the bed. Wednesday, for twelve hours, elicited one heavy sigh. By midnight Wednesday, after another long futile attempt to rouse the man, using not only psychiatric techniques but a new drug, the doctor's confidence was much diminished.

No entries, save discouraging ones, were written on his pad.

On Thursday morning, October 30, a new patient named Ernest Fitzgerald was ushered into the doctor's consulting room by Edna Willoughby.

47

Fitzgerald had called from Chicago the previous week and made his appointment through Edna. He was in the advertising business in Chicago, he said, and if Dr. Fenton could arrange to take him on, he planned to commute from Chicago for the consultations. He had been recommended by two of Dr. Fenton's former patients, whom he mentioned. He had seemed a highly intelligent and sensitive man. He was suffering, he told Edna, from loss of concentration, blackout spells and sleeplessness.

So now, entering the sunny office at 11:00 A.M. came a short and wiry blond man in his late thirties, with a pleasant smile, a sandy crew-cut and the garb of a Brooks Brothers mannequin. He had a ringing voice. He shook the doctor's hand with a firm grip. Then he sat down beside the doctor's desk, his blue eyes twinkling with appreciation.

"May I compliment you on your office, Doctor?" He glanced at the pine-paneled walls. "It's very well done. Conducive, ah—" His smile was shy. It crinkled up the lines around his eyes and drove deep lines down his cheeks, so that his face resembled a withering piece of fruit. This was a face which had probably looked old at twenty, and which would look no older at sixty. "Conducive, well—to a mental pinwheel like myself. Very fine Van Gogh," he added, looking up and past the doctor's shoulder. "I've never seen that one. May I ask if it's original?"

"Original?" The doctor smiled. "I picked it up at a bookstore for a dollar ninety-eight. Well . . ." He was very tired. New patients had always been a challenge, but it was hard to burn the candle at both ends.

Again that puckish smile, a trifle forced. The man pulled out a leather cigarette case. "Mind if I smoke? Lung cancer, what the hell. How about you?" He passed the case over. "At the moment I don't care much about the way I die." He puffed for a few moments nervously. "I work in advertising. I am a sort of writer, Doctor, an idea man."

He then went on to say, lighting a second cigarette from

the first, that he had become "all nerves" during this past month. He found it hard to concentrate. Ideas were his business, but "day after day I get out the fishing pole and not a nibble." At night he could not sleep. "My mind lights up like a ballroom." Using the trick speech of Madison Avenue or its Chicago facsimile, he kept looking at the doctor and half-smiling all the time. The effect was of a speech which had been rehearsed.

Dr. Fenton asked some routine questions.

Mr. Fitzgerald lived in Chicago, in an apartment. He had a wife. Three children, aged twelve, four, and six months. His work often brought him to New York. He had many friends in New York. Suddenly his hand, which was lighting another cigarette, began to tremble slightly. He still saw many of these friends socially. He stopped short, laid his cigarette on the ashtray, rose, paced, thrust his hand into the pocket of his tweed sports jacket, and then turned, with all the cockiness and sophistication fading from his face.

"I might as well be honest about it." He shrugged awkwardly. "This nervousness of mine has a reason. It's due to a woman."

So the doctor had already assumed. These thirty-year-old confessions, male or female, often ended up in somebody else's bed.

"A woman who at the moment is living here—in New York. I have been seeing her. She is a Mrs. Mallory?"

Here, for no reason determinable, he made the name into a question, as though, for instance, it were Zsa Zsa Gabor's, and added a quick glance to the rising inflection of his voice. But Dr. Fenton knew no Mrs. Mallory, in the gossip columns or otherwise.

Mr. Fitzgerald now returned to his wing chair, on the edge of which he perched, leaning closer to the doctor's elbow. Lowering his tone, he spoke with force.

"It is not at all what you must be thinking, Doctor. Not

49

adultery. Mrs. Mallory isn't my type. Though she is beautiful. I have no need to tell *you* that, I'm sure." He waited.

"*Me* that?" the doctor said.

Fitzgerald smiled. "She and I are friends. *Good* friends. And she has few people, believe you me, whom she can lean on. I was and am a personal friend of her sick husband. He was my roommate in Harvard, class of '42. I am referring to Dr. Eric Mallory . . . ?"

Again that rising inflection in the tone, the look of expectancy and the slight tense cock of the head. But this second name meant nothing either. Dr. Fenton frowned.

Mr. Fitzgerald now seemed disappointed. Getting off the arm of the chair, he walked to the green chaise longue, fingered it and sat down. He groped for another cigarette.

Behind him, indifferent to the hell which humans could make of living, the tropical fish swam in their big aquarium and a sunbeam slid off the tip of Beethoven's plaster nose.

"May I tell you a brief story, Doctor? It may, well, bring a certain credence to what I am about to ask." The small, dried-up face looked very earnest. "I have known Eric Mallory since our college days. He came from Cincinnati and so did I. I'd known *of* him slightly from the time I was about ten. Big wheel in Cincinnati, so I was knocked out when I found he was my roommate. He was the most brilliant fellow I'd ever met, even then. The best brain in the business. But *you* know it, Doctor. Science."

Again he paused. The doctor realized, with a certain alarm, that each pause had a significance.

"Recently I heard through friends," his visitor said, "that Eric had had a nervous breakdown, gone to pieces. I had met his wife. I was best man at their wedding," he added, with a rueful smile. "I wrote poor Angela to express my sympathy, ask what I could do. They lived, as many scientists do who work on rocket stuff, in a government-guarded town. I could not communicate with her direct. My letter was returned. It had been opened."

Dr. Fenton, to avoid those eyes, reached for a pad and fountain pen.

"I couldn't imagine, naturally, what had happened. Evidently in even knowing about poor Eric's illness, I had done something wrong. *You* know the way these people operate." He shrugged. "However, as Eric and Angela's closest friend (and we were practically like brothers, Doctor) I felt it was my duty to find out the situation. Mrs. Mallory's name had been Romagna before her marriage. I knew her family lived in Brooklyn. So, on my next trip east, I looked them up."

Mallory.

Eric.

Angela.

Brooklyn!

"Does this story you're telling me have a bearing on your symptoms, Mr. Fitzgerald?"

"I am coming to them—" Suddenly his patient smiled, and with a still more anxious look of apology, took out a handkerchief and wiped his hands. "God, I'm doing this badly. I can imagine what you think of me. Dr. Fenton," he said, "*I* have no symptoms, actually. I am not sick, except in the sense that I am sick at heart. I will admit it. This—particular call on you, this appointment was a trick."

The doctor frowned.

Fitzgerald leaped nervously to his feet. "I *had* to see you. She knows you're taking care of Eric for the General. It was she who asked me to. Begged me on her bended knees, practically, to reach you, talk to you . . ."

The doctor looked him in the eye. "Do you mean—your wife?" he asked, dead pan.

"My wife?" He laughed, an awkward, self-deprecatory laugh. "Oh—I see. I see. I sensed that this is how you'd have to react. *She* worried about it too. Angela, I mean. I said to her last week—'Angela, why don't you try to see the doctor yourself? *You* are in a better position. You're his wife. If anybody can break him down, it'll be a woman . . .' But she's shy, terribly shy. And of course they keep a constant eye on her."

"Mr. Fitzgerald." The doctor rose, trying to find control. "What you're saying is over my head. Now if you wish therapy, that's one thing, but if not . . ."

"I'm sorry, sir."

"When you're ready to discuss something I understand, you may arrange another appointment with my secretary."

His visitor remained standing sheepishly between the desk and the chaise longue.

"Then I *may* have another appointment? You aren't turning me down? A chance to talk to you about Eric is all I ask, Doctor—for *her* sake." He came forward. "Whether it's today or tomorrow or next week, any time. Anything would mean so much to her. You see, *she* doesn't know his real condition. They took him in an ambulance somewhere. She can't visit him. She gets only dry reports. She's been worrying herself sick. She doesn't know whether he's dying, whether he's permanently insane, or whether there's some hope. Could you tell me, just, whether there's hope, so I may tell her?"

"Good day, Mr. Fitzgerald."

"Aw look, Doc, I flew in all the way from Chicago. And I'm going out to Brooklyn as soon as I leave you. She's staying with her mother out near Sheepshead Bay. You can check with *her* if you please." He sat down again, looking hurt, the hurt of a perfect gentleman. For the first time, Dr. Fenton found himself weakening. This man could be bona fide. He *could* be Harvard '42, gone slightly sour. His age was the patient's age. His accent was midwestern. His clothes, his manners and his speech were not those of a movie spy.

"If it's proof you want, Dr. Fenton, I'll be happy to supply anything you ask. I know that your responsibility in regard to this is heavy. Security has us all by the tail. But let me flash some lights along the shore. One, Eric Mallory is an atomic scientist. He is our answer to the Russians . . ."

The doctor smiled what he hoped was a smile of perplexed tolerance.

"Two, he is my age, thirty-eight years old. His birthday was July twenty-ninth. He's five feet ten. Hair brown and getting bald. Wears glasses. Wife's Italian. And his little boy has asthma."

"Excuse me a second," said the doctor.

"Certainly."

Dr. Fenton walked into the reception room with some vague idea of having Edna call the Pentagon and track down the General. But Edna was at lunch. And, damn it, suppose this man *was* sincere? He certainly had showed no sign of alarm. Could "Green" afford to be trapped? It was possible, from many angles, that here *was* a decent bystander, intimately connected with the patient and his wife, who had come out of the goodness of his heart, quite stupidly, quite chivalrously.

He walked back into the consulting room.

Still bright with the noon sun, it looked as peaceful as before. His visitor was seated where he had left him. Apologetically he rose. He looked at the doctor with a subdued, defeated look, and the worried lines about his eyes and cheeks grew deeper.

"I'm afraid I've done this lousily," he said. "I've just been thinking it over. That *was* an awfully big order to ask of you. I mean, I suppose you wouldn't have given me such information, even if Eric were—one of your *regular* patients, would you?"

"I wonder if you'd care to leave a local address and phone number, Mr. Fitzgerald?"

"I'll be at Mrs. Mallory's till eight tonight. That number is Brighton 4-0669."

The doctor wrote it down.

"And your hotel?"

"I checked out an hour ago. The Romagnas are driving me to La Guardia."

"Where do you live in Chicago?"

"I've already given your secretary that. It's 40 Lakeview Apartments, Michigan Boulevard. Do you know Chicago, Doctor?"

"The phone number?"

He gave it.

"And your business address?"

"Lloyd Associates. They're a Chicago firm. It's Michigan 2-0201."

"Thank you."

"When may I come in again? If it were possible, could I bring Mrs. Mallory with me?" When the doctor stared through him, he smiled ruefully. "Still playing it cool? Well, I don't blame you. But I *don't* sleep nights. And my work is piling up. Poor little kid. What a predicament for a devoted wife. And I think she could really tell you some things that might help with your diagnosis." He paused. He shook his head. "It's not your fault. I understand. But last week when I was there . . ." He winced. "She breaks my heart."

He walked to the door and opened it. Outside, hanging on the hatrack was a fine gray hat, also a topcoat. While he put it on, he pleaded. "You couldn't give me just one word to take her—one way or another?"

"Good day, Mr. Fitzgerald."

"One tiny crumb of hope would make a difference in her life. The boy is sick again. She hasn't slept. It's hell."

"Good day," said Dr. Fenton.

"Please think it over some more. Thank you so much." He opened the door at last, then turned his head with a smile. "What is your fee, Doctor?"

"If there is one, we'll send you a bill."

Fitzgerald left, and the doctor went back into the consulting room and slumped in the wing chair. He felt as exhausted as though he'd played three sets of tennis.

The best-guarded secret of the century. Obviously. Oh

hell, yes. For a full fifteen minutes he sat there, and then he picked up the telephone and dialed long distance.

"I'd like to make a person-to-person call to Chicago," he said. "But I'll need Chicago Information for the number."

TEN

There was a copy of *Who's Who in America* on his bookshelves, and while he waited, his eyes fell on it.

"Information . . ."

"Information, we're calling for the number of Ernest Fitzgerald, 40 Lakeview Apartments, Michigan Boulevard."

In a few seconds the number was given. It tallied.

"Will you try it for me then, please?" he said.

He heard the New York operator dialing. After seven rings, he said, "I guess there's no answer."

"Would you like me to keep trying it, sir?"

"No, let's make it another number in Chicago." He gave the business number Fitzgerald had offered.

"Still person to person?"

"Please."

A man's voice answered on the first ring. "Yep?" A bit informal for an advertising agency. The operator apparently thought so too. "Is this Lloyd Associates?" she asked.

"Yep."

"Long distance calling Mr. Ernest Fitzgerald."

"He's not here, Operator." The man's voice was clipped, but refined. "Who's calling?"

"Would you see when he's expected, Operator?"

"Can you tell me when Mr. Fitzgerald is expected, please?"

"Who's calling?" the man persisted.

"New York City," the operator said.

"Look, New York City is a big place," the man said.

"Mr. Carson," the doctor said.

"Fitzgerald will be back tomorrow night." The man hung up.

Canceling the call, the doctor crossed the room to his bookshelves.

"Mallory, Eric," he read. "Physicist; b. Cincinnati, O., July 29, 1920; s. Mark and Helga (Fadjt) M; B.S., Harvard, 1942; M.S., Mass. Inst. Tech., 1943; Ph.D., U. Cal., 1944; m. Angela Romagna, 1951; 1 son, John Cavendish. With Bell Laboratories, 1945; Princeton Univ.; 1945-46; U.S. govt., 1947."

It confirmed, as though with trumpets, everything Fitzgerald had said.

The doctor sat drumming on his desk. Then he got the Brooklyn telephone book. A Victor Romagna was listed beside the telephone number Fitzgerald had given.

"Doctor . . ." Edna was standing in the doorway. "Don't you think you should get some lunch? You have an appointment in forty-five minutes?"

"How many do I have tomorrow morning?"

"Three."

"Cancel them for me, will you, please? I won't be here."

Next morning he got his car from the public garage where he kept it, inched through crosstown traffic to the West Side Highway, and then through the tunnel to Brooklyn.

It was a beautiful bright day. Even the tenements sparkled. He drove out along the edge of Bay Ridge, skirting a harbor of purest blue. Making its way toward the ocean, outlined against the hills of Staten Island, was a liner with three orange stacks. The Belt Parkway in this morning sun was quiet, relatively deserted. Curving far ahead, far off, he saw the crescent shape of Coney Island, a glittering scimitar accented by a

Ferris wheel. The air blew fresh and salt, ruffling across his hair.

Plum Beach, salt marshes, and even dunes. He was reluctant to leave these open refreshing vistas, and turn at last into crowded streets.

They were heavily populated, though peace and quiet were still here. The light fell kindly on old row houses, stores, apartment buildings, and one could still catch glimpses of the sea. Bedding hung from upstairs windows, washing flapped on the lines. Brooklyn contained cities within cities, and this section seemed like some European small town. He saw indecipherable signs on the store fronts. Bolognas, sausages, live chickens were on display. Women with dark faces wheeled baby carriages, or idled, chatting. There were few men, and they were old. He passed two bearded cronies playing chess on sidewalk chairs. He passed a goat tied up in a front yard.

And somewhere, amid all this, the wife of the greatest scientific brain in the country. If Fitzgerald was bona fide. And if he wasn't . . . ?

He slowed the car down on a quiet block, parked it and walked the rest of the way through a maze of streets. Tumble-down wooden houses, a big church, a quiet school—and there at last was the place. He paused. It was swarming with people, and the thumping noise that he had been hearing for the last three blocks proved to be the sound of a bass drum. A trumpet blasted. He saw a hearse, a line of limousines and flower cars.

A funeral.

The crowd covered the sidewalks, filled the streets. They chattered in Italian, Yiddish, Spanish, broken English. Shouldering his way in, he moved through gawking women, skipping children, crying babies, delivery boys, looking first for the address before he thought of questioning.

The address he sought was evidently the house of mourning.

All the commotion was concentrated right there. The

57

hearse stood open before the door. The man with the drum stood on the front stoop. Other musicians were milling about. It was a red-brick house like the other houses here, with a glassed-in front porch. The door of this porch was open and bore a crepe. The shades in the house were down. People kept running up and down the steps, women in black and men with mourning bands around their arms. There was a man who must be the undertaker, a frantic individual in a morning coat, a high silk hat, a white carnation in his buttonhole and a lavender hue to his complexion.

The coffin, an enormous gray one, swamped with roses, was now emerging, borne by staggering pallbearers. It was at last shoved into the silk-curtained hearse. A wail rent the air. An old lady, dressed in black, had doubled up and was sobbing openly and beating her breast. She was pacified, then shoved into one of the limousines. Many of the family already seemed to be in the cars, all in mourning, the women's faces veiled in black, but he could not see them. The shades within were drawn.

He spoke to a bystander, a woman in a velvet tam-o'-shanter.

"Whose funeral is it?"

"Oh, poor Mrs. Romagna."

"When did she die?"

"On Tuesday. The best woman that ever lived." She crossed herself. "You should have been to the wake. Even the postman came." She stood on tiptoe, craning her neck.

(*Her mother is quite ill,* the General had said.)

"Did she have any children?" he asked the lady.

"Sure. Eight." She held up two hands. "One came here all the way from California. Oh, there you are, Rosie." She clutched a friend. "Say, did you ever see so many flowers? They say the casket cost three thousand dollars. These Italians!"

Why hadn't Ernest Fitzgerald mentioned death?

The doctor was pushed and shoved now back and forth.

The band, with more desultory toots and thumps, was lining up. Dressed in business suits, they formed a phalanx, after the chief undertaker had rearranged them several times. Then they began to play, an off-key rendition of Beethoven's Funeral March, arranged for cornets, tuba and the drum. The effect of the music was strange, so early in the morning, on this noisy street.

But the crowd fell silent, as the flower cars and the hearse began to move.

And behind the hearse, on foot, marched the male members of the family, in coal-black suits, carrying their hats across their hearts. They paced with gravity and expressions of deep sorrow (some wept) to the thumping of the drum, the slow, sad melancholy of the tune. It was old world and in its own way quite splendid.

Limousine after limousine departed, each one speculatively examined by the doctor. Angela Mallory, one of eight children, should be in one. And she was beautiful, fantastically attractive. But he could distinguish nothing. The veils were thick, the shades stayed down.

He addressed another fascinated face, an open-mouthed youth in a rubber apron.

"Which one is Mrs. Mallory, the pretty daughter?"

The boy turned round, his mouth still open.

"I *hear* she's pretty," the doctor said, smiling.

The youth shrugged awkwardly. Then, smiling, he broke into Spanish, from which, using his small command of that language, the doctor judged that the speaker was a stranger here himself. He had just been passing in a diaper truck which was parked beyond.

The last limousine had left. And in the distance, not too far away, a church bell began to toll above the resounding music of the band. The funeral, by foot and by car, was crawling toward the church. The crowd was following. Drawn with it, the doctor drifted on. He caught up with the cars again, and once more scrutinized the limousines. Mrs. Romagna might have been a millionaire, or a gangster's mother, to judge by all this display. He asked more questions.

Was one of Mrs. Romagna's daughters named Angela?

He found at last that one of them was.

Was she a married daughter?

She was. All the Romagna girls were married.

Was her name Mallory?

Did she have a son?

The questionee did not know, or did not stop to answer. The spectacle was too engrossing, morbidly glamorous. The doctor had heard it said that in the milestone events of life, Italians were extravagant.

The band and hearse had reached a church, a big gray edifice with a clanging bell. High Mass was evidently next on the agenda. Now the limousines were being emptied. The doctor stood with bared head, watching.

An old man with a cane hobbled out.

After him came a child, a little girl dressed all in black from head to toe. She even carried a black-edged handkerchief, rather self-importantly, he noted.

Then came three women, shrouded figures, one very tall, one medium, one fat. These in the first car ought to be the daughters of the deceased. The woman in the middle, the medium one, had pretty ankles. Her breasts were full, voluptuous. But he could not glimpse her face.

She paused one moment on the steps of the church, speaking to a friend. And so intent was the doctor on this pause that he almost missed the lady in the second car.

She too wore full mourning, the waist-length veil, a plain black coat, black stockings. She was clasping the hand of a small pale little boy. He could be about four years of age. He was dressed in a gray cap, gray shorts and knee socks, like an English child.

She removed his cap, revealing light-brown hair, as they approached the steps of the church. Under the full black coat, it was impossible to see her figure, but her legs were slim and shapely. She held her head high and with dignity. Nor could he see beneath the clinging crepe of the veil. And yet he had the impression of beauty, as she passed him. Something soft, yet regal, the manner of a princess.

He had not thought of "Angela Mallory" as regal. Something more voluptuous and more blatant seemed to go with pinups. But beauty, like genius, did not always flaunt itself. And that boy might have had a grandmother with a name like Helga.

He turned away from the church, and walked back to the car, wondering.

At dusk he sat again in his office, waiting for Edna to leave. When she had finally done so, he dialed the number. By now the body would have been laid to rest. By now even so elaborate a funeral as that one should be over.

"Hello." It was a male voice; in the background many other voices and the clatter of silverware.

"May I speak to Mrs. Mallory, please?"

The phone was set down, and he heard a voice calling, "Angie . . ."

And presently a soft, musical "Yes?"

"Mrs. Mallory?"

"Yes, this is Mrs. Mallory."

"I am trying to reach a Mr. Ernest Fitzgerald. He told me he might be visiting you this evening."

"Ernest Fitzgerald?" There was a vulnerable, almost child-like innocence and politeness to the reply. "Why no, as a matter of fact, I haven't seen him for years."

"Oh, I see."

"He was my husband's roommate in Harvard," she went on. "In fact, he was best man at our wedding, but he lives in Chicago. I believe he—" Belatedly she checked herself, but the afterthought was still polite. "Who's calling, please?"

"I'm sorry to have disturbed you," the doctor said. "Thank you."

He hung up. For a while longer he sat at his desk.

A phony, then. Mr. Ernest Fitzgerald was a phony. But to what extent a phony?

The doctor walked to the window, looked down into the lighted canyons of the city. It was dark by now. A crescent moon floated above the Waldorf.

A dangerous phony without doubt. And a very knowledgeable phony, who had led him (for God knows what murky reasons) straight to the wife of the patient.

And from the standpoint of professional curiosity, what a temptation it was to go to see her, talk with one who sounded so refined and gentle, get her to shed light on what had driven her husband insane.

Brooklyn was temptingly close.

But that was out of the question. He had made solemn promises.

The more critical question was whether he should report the events of the past two days to the General. From the standpoints of honor, of obedience, the answer was clearly yes.

He turned away from the window, remembering the General's positiveness in saying that if it should be decided that he, Fenton, was in danger, he would be automatically removed from the case.

He did not want to be removed from the case. Somehow he did not believe in the danger. He would take the responsibility for keeping silent. He would take the risk and see what happened next.

But after his return from Base X, falling exhausted into bed, he had thought it over, and was maligning himself for egotism of the rankest sort. To assume that his own personal safety was the only thing at stake was vainglory. To take matters into his own hands out of some misguided sense of heroism could very easily prejudice the safety of that woman, as well as the security of the United States.

He would tell the General, even if it meant removal from

the case. At least it would mean that he'd be getting a lot more sleep. But it was important to tell the General himself. Not Stevens, not the underlings. He would ask Stevens to arrange another meeting.

ELEVEN

"Wichita Falls . . ." The patient's voice was clear and distinct.

And then: ". . . the face of the earth."

After a grueling flight, the doctor sat in the red room, listening to the tape recorder. Its use as a watchdog in the intervals between his visits had borne fruit.

"That was on Saturday afternoon," said Major Brown, consulting a note pad.

And at four o'clock on Sunday, November 2, the patient had said, in the manner of a college professor lecturing a class:

"Science is beyond this pettiness, gentlemen. I respect no rules except the rules of mathematics. Look to the stars. Do they contend among themselves?"

There was gagging after this, and a marked inability to speak. Then he cried out, as though in pain, "What have *I* done?"

At eight o'clock that night, after a period of sleep, he had begun a lecture on radiation waves.

This evidently had contained too much of the technical, for it was highly censored. Long gaps occurred in the tapes where the Major had done some cutting. But enough was there to be impressive.

The erudition of this man still seemed intact.

Here was a brain still aware professionally. The patient spoke quite calmly and with perfect enunciation for quite a while, moving through the cosmic heavens as though they were a well-mapped highway.

"The moon must be regarded only as a stepping stone. Here we can refuel . . ."

Was this "insanity" or the world of a different breed of men, men who in the space of a few brief years had made strange dreams come true, and were pushing further on to a limitless conquest of Time? Men who regarded Earth and its brief history as a jumping-off point and the moon as a mere filling station.

The patient seemed neither militant nor nationalistic in his ideas. He did not talk about "bases," a race, or chauvinistic possession of the planets. As far as could be determined (though Major Brown might have censored much) his attitude toward space travel was nonpolitical, almost personal. He wanted to devise equipment and explore a road. That was all.

On Monday morning, November 3, the day when Dr. Fenton was again due, he had tossed and muttered.

Only a few words were distinct. Once again the mysterious "Wichita Falls." He was obsessed with that town. The doctor had looked it up in the Britannica, and checked its possible significance with Major Brown. It was a town in Texas, population 68,042, near the Oklahoma border, on Wichita River. Major Brown said there was no government base there. Nor, so far as anyone knew, had the patient ever lived there.

"Now," said Dr. Throckmorton, beginning to gurgle with excitement, "listen to what's coming next."

Dr. Fenton listened, and heard the patient ask the time and day of the week. With pleased surprise, the orderly replied that it was seven o'clock in the evening, Monday, November 3.

The patient then mentioned Dr. Fenton's name and asked if this were not the night when the doctor was due to arrive.

He said this with considerable effort and whispered tones, but he had the name correct. Thus it was evident that by now the doctor's comings and goings had registered. Memory and some orientation were present.

Throckmorton beamed. Major Brown snapped off the set. "That's about it," he said.

"Good," said Dr. Fenton. "Well, let's get started then, shall we?"

He looked at his watch. It was close to eleven, almost too late to start. They had been lucky to make it to Base X at all. Winds of almost gale intensity had buffeted the plane the entire way. For a while Stevens had favored turning back. They had arrived an hour later than usual.

The doors rolled back.

"Good evening. I am Dr. Fenton . . ."

The patient ignored this greeting. But he was awake, and rather violently awake, for very shortly after the doctor's voice had died away, some heavy breathing began, and the now familiar choking, gasping sounds which heralded an outburst. Dr. Fenton waited.

"I can't go through with it!" the patient cried suddenly, then paused.

"Through with what?" the doctor asked quietly.

"*You* don't know," was the fierce reply. Not addressed to him, he thought, but to some vision. "My back is to the wall." This ended in a sort of gasp, a whimper, then the sounds of tossing came through the microphones, the rustling of sheets.

"Is that your wife to whom you're speaking?" asked the doctor.

Instantly, almost warily, the tossing ceased. There was a long, long silence. With sudden sharpness, directly, the question came.

"Do you know my wife?" the patient asked.

"No. We have never met," the doctor said. "But I have heard about her. And she is safe. So is your boy."

"They aren't. You're a liar. Excuse me." Cultured and yet

explosive, the refined voice now came tightly. As through set teeth he groaned, "Oh, God! Oh, God! What fools!"

"They are safe, my friend."

But this did not calm him. Thrashing about in the bed, he seemed to be beating his head against a pillow. "Idiot," he groaned. "So stupid."

He paused. Fear seemed to have overcome him once again, and for about five minutes he remained as silent as a statue. Dr. Fenton now spoke soothingly.

He explained that the woman and the child were under constant protection, as was the patient too. Every effort was being made to preserve his home, and it would be there when he returned. That was, if the patient wished it to be there. Repeating all the General's bromides (for there was nothing he dared add) he emphasized the earnest desire of the state to please the patient at any cost. The state assumed that he loved his family. It was a part of him. And so he must not fear for it.

"Would you like to hear from your wife?" he asked.

"Come here. *You!*" the patient said. "*You.* Out there. *Closer.*"

The doctor slowly rose from his chair. The hairs on the back of his neck had risen. The voice was low, conspiratorial, intimate.

"Closer." It was a whisper now.

It was impossible to get any closer. His nose was almost touching the canvas of the screen. He was so close, that if he pushed a little, he could probably touch that bed. He could hear the breathing beyond, unamplified. He could almost feel the movements of the lips, the eyes fixed on him.

"Are you as close as possible?"

"I am as close as possible. What do you want to tell me?"

"I want you to . . . to . . . Don't let them close the doors!"

"I won't. What is it?"

"Take us to the moon," came the disappointing reply, still

whispered desperately. "You tell them that. That's where we'll all be safe. Only on the moon—"

"Your wife and son?"

"Yes?" Sibilantly, with panic. "Nobody has reached it yet. Or have they?"

"Not yet."

"Not in *my* ship. Nobody knows about *my* ship. My special ship. But I've got one in my desk. Don't close the doors!" he shouted. He whispered, "Do you know where she is?"

"No, sir."

"Oh!" A deep, disappointed sigh. Then— "Are you brave?'

"I try to be," Dr. Fenton said.

"How old are you?"

"Forty-two."

"Are you married?"

"No."

"What do you do?"

"Psychiatry. Helping worried people."

"Psychiatry! Hmph!" There was a loud sound of disgust. "*I've* talked to them. They're know-nothings. Psychiatry isn't *science*. Can you measure a dream?"

"No. Not measure. But maybe judge."

"Do you know what makes men into devils?"

"Sometimes," said Dr. Fenton.

"To you there are no devils."

"I believe that evil people exist, and can do harm."

"And I am evil. Do you think that?"

"Not at all. Just troubled."

"Troubled!" The patient laughed, a harsh, wild laugh. "I'm an evil bastard, that's what I am. I'm a murdering devil. I'm damned. Why don't you shoot me? All of you. Shoot me!" he cried so that the prisms in the chandeliers began to ring. "You all have guns!" He began to sob.

"Nobody wants to shoot you."

"Liar!"

"Tell me who does?"

The sobs went on, finally dwindling down to a sigh.

"Will you tell me sometime?"

But the patient's interest seemed to have wandered off. He began muttering and tossing, and again was heard the fateful name of Wichita Falls. Nobody stirred in the big bare room.

"What happened at Wichita Falls?"

Just muttering.

"Will you tell me sometime?" the doctor asked.

"Yes."

"When I come back on Wednesday?"

The patient did not answer.

"We want to help you find those devils," Dr. Fenton said. "We don't want you to be shot. We want you to be happy."

He paused. The screen was silent.

"But you must help us. Only *you* can help us. We are your friends. Do you believe that?"

"Yes," the patient said. "Yes . . ." Very slowly, tentatively. "Yes, Doctor . . . Fenton . . ."

It was a most cheerful set of faces that surrounded him after the doors were closed. Dr. Throckmorton chortled and patted him on the back. Major Brown proposed a drink, and brought out a bottle of bourbon. Even the imperturbable Stevens looked pleased. Wonderful, amazing seemed the play to this long-suffering audience, and many questions were asked, each point rehashed. Did the doctor realize that the patient not only knew his name, but *liked* him? And how about the marked improvement in speech, the lucidity of those sentences?

How could they help till the next session? They were ready to stand on their heads to play some part in speeding up the cure. Their fate depended upon that cure, and Base X had long ago lost all its novelty. Dr. Throckmorton's arthritis had reappeared. Major Brown had an infected wisdom tooth.

Dr. Fenton felt pleased. This was a big advance, a break, but they had a long, long way to go. The patient had opened up, showed intelligence, some awareness, some warmth of human feeling and the beginning of trust, but he was a very sick man, irrational, paranoid, fantasy-ridden, and the source of his dilemma as yet unknown. Whether his problem was personal, political, real or unreal still remained to be discovered, and after discovery, treatment must begin. That treatment, considering that the mind itself was of extraordinary caliber, would be a ticklish job. It might take months.

But he threw no wet blanket on their enthusiasm. He drank his bourbon, participated in the toasts. Only when he got outside (it was long after one) and, blindfolded, faced the storm, the slippery bridge, the mud, did he give way to gloom. And then it was not the storm or the dreary weeks of wintry weather which oppressed him. Storms could be outfaced, but he had other reasons for wanting a quick cure. Why had the patient thought his *wife* was going to be murdered?

Perhaps "devils" did exist.

In this morning's mail another letter from Green had come, with a New Jersey telephone number. Last night his office safe and files had been broken into. And when, during the flight down, he had asked Stevens to let him see the General, he had been told that it would be at least two days before a meeting could be arranged.

TWELVE

The storm had not abated, and it was after 4:00 A.M. when the plane arrived at Newark. Dutybound, he left the cab as usual at 86th Street and walked toward his house. The streets were rivers, black and wind-swept. Rain ran in rivulets from his hat. He was very tired and very wet, and perhaps it was illusion, the effect of so much suspense, but he had the sense that he was being followed.

The nondescript bulk of a man had definitely stepped from under an awning as he turned west on Lexington. And, glancing back from time to time, he saw that this figure kept pace half a block away. By 92nd and Madison, the shadow was still visible, coming inexorably on. Maybe a drunk. But the silence of the pre-dawn city, the whistling wind and the old-fashioned, unlit houses made a sullen framework for the figure.

But he was not accosted. And, seeing his house at last, he now had another worry to drive this one away. The front-room lights were blazing.

Always, on the other late nights, Louisa had left only a dim light in the hall. As he got out his key on the stoop, the door was opened and her bathrobed figure confronted him.

"Doctor, where have you been? I was ready to call the police. There's been a sick man here all night."

"A sick man. Who?"

"He said he was a patient of yours. He said your answering service wouldn't tell him where you were. And he didn't want to go to a hospital. So he came right here. Oh, look at your *overcoat.* Have you been *walking?* In that rain?"

"What's his name? Is he upstairs?"

He had already glanced into the lighted parlor. It was empty.

"Oh no. Finally he went away. A Mr. Fitzgerald. Ernest Fitzgerald."

Slowly he took off his hat and shook it. Then he walked on sopping feet into the parlor.

"How long was he here?"

"He came around nine. He waited and waited and waited. Finally I told him not to wait any more."

"And when was that?"

"Around one."

Cigarette butts overflowed the coffee-table ashtray, several other ashtrays were also filled. But there were not any visible signs of outrage. Damn. Not to be able to warn *her*.

Not to be permitted even to show his alarm to this old friend, the guardian of his home. And the General, as yet, no help.

"Did he leave an address?"

"No, he said you knew it."

Her description of the visitor matched the description of last Thursday's "patient" exactly, except that the man tonight had not been calm. He had had a crew-cut, was short, blond, very well dressed, but looked very pale, and was shaking, when Louisa opened the door. Deeply apologetic and with a tremor in his voice, he had told her that he hadn't slept at all for the last three nights, and was at the very end of his rope. She had built him a fire in the library, and later offered him a cup of tea. This, of course, was one of the maddening factors of the business, for patients *had* been offered similar refuge before. Indeed, as the maternal type and curious, Louisa tried her best to be in on the doctor's professional affairs, and she reveled in such opportunities to hear case histories, offer consolation and act as liaison. She was very jealous of Edna Willoughby.

"How much did you talk to him?"

He was still moving about the rooms, opening drawers, glancing at the contents, but nothing seemed to have been disturbed.

"Not very much. He said the fire was very restful. So I just looked in on him from time to time."

"You gave him the run of the house?"

"Not really. But where were *you* so late?"

Exhausted by the events of the night before, the doctor overslept, arrived at his office later than his first appointment, and it was still raining hard. A three-day northeaster seemed in prospect. The heat was on, the office far too hot. Edna

Willoughby kept bothering him about the office "robbery" (she felt that the building superintendent should be notified, if he insisted on keeping it from the police) and the files were still mixed up. He found himself listening to patients without much interest, his ears alerted only when the phone rang.

He badly wanted to hear from Operator 10.

Between one and two, while he was out to lunch, another curious thing happened. He found the message typed by Edna on his desk when he returned.

"A lady called. Potential patient, says she. Too nervous to make appointment here. Would like to meet you instead at six tonight in Hotel Astor lobby. Wouldn't leave her name or address. Asks you wear white flower in lapel. She'll wear a red camellia."

He burst out laughing. And it was a relief to laugh. Slippery Fitzgeralds, robberies and Mr. Green's special deliveries and phone numbers, and now—Mata Hari. They weren't even subtle.

He crumpled up the memo, tossed it into the wastebasket.

At four Stevens finally telephoned.

"This is Operator 10. Are you alone? Please ask your secretary to get off the line." Considering how many people now seemed to be in on all the "secrets," it was amusing to hear old Stony Stevens sticking to his guns.

But the doctor obeyed.

"Okay?"

"Okay."

"The General will see you at Base X tomorrow evening. He has heard that latest tape. He is delighted."

"Thanks."

What with shadowy figures and red camellias, the triumph of last night seemed now like ancient history.

"Newark. Same time. Tomorrow night." Stevens hung up.

Till then he was on his own. Still a day and a half before he could tell the General.

As the afternoon wore on, the doctor fished the memo from the trash basket, read it again, and then asked Edna about the phone call.

"She sounded more frightened than anything else," Edna said. "She talked in very low tones, as though she was afraid somebody might hear her."

"Hmm," he said.

"Doctor . . ." Edna was seated at her typewriter. She looked up at him candidly. "Are you all right?"

He smiled. "Of course," he said.

"This isn't the place I once knew," she said. "Frankly I'm beginning to feel more like a secretary to some private eye . . . have you changed your name to Queen, by any chance?"

Again he smiled. "It's occurred to me, Edna, that this might be a good time for you to take your vacation. What do you think? I mean a bonus vacation. You'll still have one coming in the summer."

"Why?"

"I just think it might be a good idea. Certain things I don't want you to risk . . . I mean get involved with . . ."

"You mean it's dangerous for me to be working here?"

"I don't really know," he said. "It might be."

"Hmm," she said. She shook the auburn curls. "If there's excitement I want to be in on it."

"I wish you'd think about it," he said. "In any case I don't want you staying here after closing hours. No overtime work."

"I was never much of a one for that anyway. Doctor . . ." She paused. "Do you mind if I tell you that you look terrible?"

"I know," he said.

"Are you going to meet that crazy woman at the Astor?"

"I don't think so," he said. "Frankly I think I'll go home and go to sleep."

He allowed extra time for getting a cab and, bizarrely enough, got one immediately, so that it was still ten minutes before six when he entered the Astor lobby.

73

But not with a white flower in his buttonhole. To hell with that. In the first place he didn't like flowers in his lapel, and in the second place there was no point in *telegraphing* his identity.

He went first to the newsstand and bought a pack of cigarettes and a copy of the *World-Telegram*, then crisscrossed the lobby and walked once about its perimeter. No red camellias. Women meeting for dinner and the theater; an old lady dozing; men looking from newspapers to watches and back to newspapers; bellhops struggling with luggage. It was a busy place, a favorite meeting spot for out-of-towners. The revolving doors never came to rest. But no women with red camellias.

He waited, leaning against a pillar. Finally a chair was vacated. It faced the Broadway entrance. He took it, settling down behind his newspaper, looking every few seconds at the revolving doors. Five minutes passed.

At precisely six o'clock, a tall, well-built redhead emerged from the revolving doors, crossed to the newsstand, then strolled into the lobby proper, stopping a few feet away from where he sat. She looked at the big clock; she scanned the lobby. Her lips moved. He caught her eye. She looked haughtily away. She wore a white camellia—or was it a gardenia? He could never tell the damned things apart. In any case, it was not red.

Catching her eye again, he rose. "May I offer you my seat?"

"My goodness, such chivalry." Smiling, she sat down. "Thank you, dear."

She was up again immediately, saying "Lester!" and advancing to meet a man in a camel's-hair coat that was far too long for him. They linked arms and left.

Dr. Fenton took the chair again, raised the newspaper. Again he looked about the lobby. Almost every woman in the place was wearing a flower of some kind. He had never realized how many women wore flowers. Junior Prom night at the Hotel Astor.

And to compound the uncertainty, making the rounds of the lobby came a man in a shabby topcoat, carrying a basket of white flowers. A placard attached to the basket said "50 cents."

It was by now six-fifteen. Somebody had gotten cold feet.

He returned to his newspaper, this time becoming engrossed in a story concerning juvenile delinquency. When he next looked at the clock, it was almost six-twenty, and scanning the lobby again, he saw a woman he had not noticed before. She sat on an opposite sofa, her back to the revolving doors. She was more a girl than a woman, a pretty slim brunette. If she had been there before, he would have noticed her, no doubt of that.

But she wore no flower, white or red.

He returned briefly to his newspaper, then looked again. Red camellia or not, she was worth looking at. Delicately made and graceful, she was all in black. But it was not the chic costume or the figure that held his eye, but the face above it. A face too romantic almost for the fashionable suit, the small black velvet hat. A face like a Murillo Virgin. Gentle, classic, with modest, downcast eyes.

As he watched, she crossed her legs, putting one slim ankle on display.

He lost interest in the newspaper and looked just for the sheer pleasure of looking, glancing away only often enough to avoid outright staring, and to check the doors.

When he turned his eyes to her face again, she was looking directly at him. Her eyes were a remarkable brown, large and velvety, with a look so candid as to seem childlike. He smiled. She looked away.

It was now six-twenty-five.

For God's sake, he thought, maybe red camellias were out of season. Maybe there weren't any red camellias. Maybe the truck bringing red camellias had broken down in Hoboken.

He rose and crossed to where she sat.

"Good evening," he said. "Was it you who called?"

She looked at him blankly, or perhaps it was feigned blankness. Then color flooded her face. Her lips moved, but it was a murmur rather than an answer.

"I am Dr. Fenton," he said.

She smiled, with deep embarrassment, and softly shook her head. Then she dropped her eyes to her purse.

"I'm terribly sorry," he said, and returned to his chair, this time making no pretense of reading the newspaper.

She was now scanning the room, the low chignon moving gracefully as she turned her head, first this way and then that. Her eyes avoided him consistently. Frowning, she looked at the clock. What a beautiful woman. Not a feature, not a gesture that was not feminine, subtly alluring. Once more her eyes met his, and this time they had a look of softness . . . of apology.

She was rising and walking gracefully toward the revolving doors.

He followed her.

When he got through the doors, she was already down on the sidewalk. He saw her toss something into the gutter, then move off into the rainy night amidst the dinner-hour crowds.

He paused long enough to look. There in the gutter was a crumpled flower, its color a bright red.

A passing taxi immediately ran over it, splashing mud against his trousers. And down Broadway, nothing was to be seen except a host of faces, many umbrellas moving like a river under the rain, the glittering signs.

THIRTEEN

The room with the red Chinese wallpaper looked different when the doctor's blindfold was removed on Wednesday night. Two large wing chairs had been set before the fireplace, with a braided rug between them; a fire had been laid and a handsome antique silver coffee service set upon a pie-crust table to the right of the mantel.

The General was in uniform, impressive, amiable, though his wavy white hair and waxen countenance under the glaring globe lights made him look more than ever like an old-fashioned tailor's dummy. He wrung Dr. Fenton's hand, but did not sit down.

"I should like to have our talk *after* the session, Doctor. Tonight I intend to listen in. It should be an interesting evening, eh? Hope that's all right with you?"

"Of course," the doctor said.

"I was more than impressed with your work the other night." The rolling tone was, as usual, ministerial. "You hit the mark in that last tape. And the boys here tell me that he has been more than co-operative. Well, I won't keep you. Do you want to speak to Throckmorton?"

"Just briefly . . ."

So it was going to be a command performance. Excitement was in the air. Dr. Throckmorton, when he came in, was more than ever erect and immaculate. He had abandoned his cane. Even the screen itself looked whiter tonight, as though it had been scrubbed for the occasion. Dr. Throckmorton said that the patient had allowed his "mask" to be changed, and that he had been bathed and shaved without much fuss.

"He is so *much* better since you were here. Dazed, and still suspicious of us all, to be sure. But I honestly think he's coming out of it. He didn't carry on a mite when the General came in to inspect the room, but just lay there watching him. And he has twice since Monday asked about *you*."

"Has the major kept on the microphones?"

"Oh yes. But nothing new has developed. He has stopped talking about Wichita Falls and murder, if that is what you

77

mean. It's all been very peaceful. I suspect that he is saving everything for *you*."

High flattery, though the doctor privately would have preferred less. It threw too great a responsibility on his shoulders, but worse than that, all these preparations might shrink the patient's willingness to talk. This was a confession chamber, not a stage, and he wished as well that the General had not chosen to appear in that sickroom. At best it was a change in normal routine.

But the carefully oiled doors slid open. And, trying to establish at once a familiar atmosphere, he addressed the glistening canvas.

There was no reply to anything for a good twenty minutes.

He went through all his book of tricks again. He explained the General's presence tonight as a sign of faith and hope. He spoke of the love the country bore the patient, the future protection that would be given him. He spoke of science and its aims, the charms of family life, the tender concern of the patient's wife and child. Tonight, he added, he would try to arrange with the General for some kind of correspondence between them now. At this, at last, there came a kind of yawn, and then a quiet chuckle.

"P-poor Fenton." The voice beyond was almost affectionate in its tone, but choking as before. "Y-you try so hard."

"I am here to help."

Long pause.

"Y-*you* . . . do help," came the grudging compliment. "Only—you . . . Perhaps . . ." He paused. Then he said, with irritation and with a return somewhat to the incomprehensible rapid-fire delivery of an earlier stage, "Whatthehell—isthebrassforhere—tonight?"

"The General is my boss," the doctor said. "He has employed me to help you."

"H-help me? He'd court-martial me." Restless thrashing. Five minutes of it. "The-the-the-the-microphones!" he said, with a marked return of the speech block. "Night and dd-d-

78

day. No privacy. Wh-wh-why can't you and I? . . . In here . . . I—I—"

"Yes. Take it easy," Dr. Fenton said, moving closer to the screen. "I'm close."

"I *could* spill . . . lots . . ." Almost indistinguishable now, the voice trailed off to silence.

And there it remained.

What things, for instance?

Wichita Falls? Something to do with Wichita Falls, the doctor asked.

Had something terrible happened in Wichita Falls?

The patient had evidently panicked, or was stubbornly on strike against the General. He was the star in the spotlight, but tonight he had turned temperamental, and maybe this was good. It showed an awareness of the circumstances and the routine. Also, it showed the patient's growing partiality—for just one man, Dr. Fenton. For, at the very end, after eleven o'clock, when the audience in the wings undoubtedly was cursing the fiasco, he added just one thing (as though he were also conscious of the time and them).

"You're a good guy, Doctor . . . Come back . . . *Next* time."

The doors rolled shut at eleven twenty-five.

But poor as the "show" had been, the General seemed pleased. He came marching back into the room, followed by the bustling staff and an orderly bearing a heap of firewood. The General seemed intent on making up for the sparse hospitality of the Hotel Bennington, and besides the coffee, Scotch and brandy were also brought in. He liked a fire, he said, snapping out the four big lights after the staff had finally departed. It was as comforting to a man's soul as reading a chapter in the Good Book—and since, unfortunately, they could not permit the doctor to enter any other room in this house, he had conceived the idea of cheering up this room in here. This fireplace hadn't been used in years, and the house was frame,

79

but the boys had cleaned out the flues and removed some ivy overgrowing the top of the chimney.

"Well now. Stevens tells me that you have some questions . . ."

They at last got down to brass tacks, sitting opposite each other in the big blue chairs, the flames casting a warm and ruddy light. The room once more took on an eighteenth-century atmosphere, with its ghostly mirror and its crystal chandelier. It was a strange transition.

"Yes, I do have questions—and problems," Dr. Fenton began. Lighting another cigarette, he then told the General all that had occurred: Fitzgerald's first visit to his office, the facts that had been disclosed, the mysterious ransacking of his files, Fitzgerald's visit to his home, his trip to Brooklyn, his encounter with the pretty girl at the Hotel Astor. He left out nothing, made a clean breast of his feelings and his acts. All the time he watched the General's face, particularly when the name of Eric Mallory was introduced.

But even his trained eye could detect very little in that scarred and repaired countenance shadowed in the wing of the big chair.

When he had finished, there was silence, broken only by the crackle and hiss of the flames.

"I don't know what to believe even now," the doctor said. "The ransacking of my safe, of course, seems the only *dangerous* thing which has occurred. But it might have nothing to do with spies. That building has often been robbed. Nothing was taken. And Mr. Fitzgerald *could* be bona fide, although I very much doubt it. Frankly, I hesitate telling on people who might have honorable motives but who are simply behaving stupidly . . ." Again he paused.

"No . . ." The General formed the word very carefully, and with rounded lips. "I'm glad you told me, although I'm sorry it had to happen." He rose and poked at the fire. "It must make us look very weak, if not downright careless." With his back turned to the doctor, he almost mumbled the next few words. "Espionage has become a science. And in a case like this . . . wheels within wheels . . ."

"Then it *was* espionage?"

"I believe it was." The General gravely turned, standing before the mantel and again looking like a dominie, a bemused and solemn one, searching for a prayer. His eyes looked over the rimless glasses, which had slid slightly down upon his fleshy nose. "Some of it was. I don't believe in Mr. Fitzgerald, in any case. The patient's college roommate is not in this country."

"But the addresses in Chicago?"

"The apartment number could have been registered under another name or be the actual address of a bona-fide Mr. Fitzgerald who is not living there at present. They have a dozen tricks with phone numbers, Fenton." He sighed and fumbled in his pocket, producing an extraordinarily small notebook. "I am more interested in the man who answered at the business number. That has more point. Do you recall that number?"

The doctor produced it; he had kept a record. The General wrote it down.

"Lloyd Associates. I'll check the address. Though it's probably too late now."

"I am sorry, sir. I am new at this. And," Dr. Fenton could not resist saying in self-defense, "I have no way of *immediately* contacting you."

The General simply frowned into his notebook. He held his pencil poised.

"This woman and the man. Could you describe them, please?"

When the doctor had complied with this request in detail, and he had scribbled everything down, the General still stood there with a worried frown.

"Curious," he muttered to himself, then resumed his seat. He tapped the notebook against his knee. "And this man said that he was leaving from La Guardia that same night?"

"Yes, sir. And that the Romagnas were driving him to the

airport." The doctor paused. "Though the Mallory woman didn't know a thing about it, hadn't seen him. Am I to assume"—again the doctor hesitated—"that the proper names were given? The lady in Brooklyn didn't sound like a phony."

The General picked up his coffee, stirred it. "Doctor, it would be wiser for you to assume nothing in this case. Neither now, nor later." He sat down heavily, a gloomy man sipping coffee, and the firelight luridly lit up a line of stitches beneath one ear. "We cannot be precipitate." He turned, looking directly at the doctor now, and laid the coffee cup on the floor. "The problem is far graver. As it must already have occurred to you, this poses a very melancholy decision for me."

"The danger point?" asked Dr. Fenton.

"Precisely." The General once more stood up. A man of few nerves, he revealed them now in the sudden thrust of his big hands into his jacket pockets and the sucking in of his big lower lip. He began to pace between the two wing chairs. "You are obviously vulnerable now. Everything about you is known, including the time your secretary goes out to lunch, the hours when you are here, your home address. God knows how they hit the mark, but they have, and they are going to make you their prime target."

"But Mr. Green knew all about me weeks ago," the doctor murmured. "And you—"

The General waved his hand impatiently. "Whoever these people are, they are an organization, with money, offices around the country, clever personnel. And any trick might be tried." He paused before the fireplace. "You are a doctor. You have to be available to the public. Any stranger could walk into your consulting room. Or some fake patient could lure you to an address. I couldn't guard you without attracting undue attention. I cannot ask you to close up shop. You cannot warn your secretary or your maid to be on guard against them. So . . ." He stopped, his expression as dejected as though the bars had just been stripped from his chest. His voice grew sad. "I had hoped to keep you on until our man was well. After tonight it seems more vital than ever that you should be kept on. But—" he shrugged—"they have struck you off the list."

So there it was, the end that he had feared. Loss of the case and the patient, whom he had come to like, who was an enormous challenge, and who, after weeks of patience, had finally evinced some signs of trust. Medicine must go down before a lot of greedy, slippery criminals. Perhaps science itself would suffer. Perhaps the future of the United States.

"Does the danger involved mean danger for the country or simply danger to myself?" he asked the General. "Because, well, frankly I'm not disturbed."

The General fingered his lip.

"Does my knowing who they are, and their knowing about me affect Security *deeply?* Does it affect the safety of the patient?"

"No. I cannot fathom their total motives. They seem foolish on the one hand, and very clever on the other." Once more the General paced. "But they are probably trying to get through you to the patient, determine where he is, what his condition is . . . That, I am quite positive, they can't know, or that sandy-haired fellow wouldn't have showed up twice. Nor would the girl have called you." Less downcast, more excited, the General picked up his coffee once more. "Obviously the home visit and the ransacking of your files was another crude attempt. But they'll get cruder. And more desperate than sending women with red flowers." He stopped, laid the coffee down. "That was a peculiar thing, that flower business. I still don't get the pitch. Why the hell didn't she put the flower on? You say you spoke to her?"

"Yes, but, General, I'm not sure she was the woman. The flower in the gutter might have been coincidence."

"Some fat coincidence. You saw her throw it, didn't you? What was she after?" He frowned and shook his head. "Crazy. There you were—the setup perfect . . ."

"Not perfect, sir." The doctor reddened. "I intended to

obey the rules." He spoke more forcefully. "Am I to assume that I am to take no chances, make no decisions in these matters? At the time all that I did was with the hope of helping you. Meeting these people so I could learn a little."

The General seemed deep in thought. He did not answer.

"Am I to assume as well," Dr. Fenton went on, "that calling Mrs. Mallory in Brooklyn was also wrong?"

Still the General did not answer. He stared off at the shadows.

"Is Eric Mallory the patient's name?"

"Doctor . . ." The General smiled wanly, though his face was still in shadow, back-lighted by the fire's glow. "There are many important scientists in the United States. Why press the point right now? It is better not to know."

"But it would help—"

"Help you with what? Only to reach persons who, if they have information, can give it through the proper channels. Which we, in turn, will gladly pass to you. All the rest, my boy, lies in the danger zone. I thought I had made that clear. We are keeping this man anonymous to help *you*, not help ourselves. Why, if I had a choice, I'd take you in there, let you meet him tonight. But I can't. Off or on the case, you must be thoroughly protected."

"But these criminals know his name."

"You don't know that for a fact, Fenton. Have I confirmed it? Has any report you've read confirmed it? Not knowing it for a *fact* is all that actually might save you. Oh, you don't know these bastards. They can wash your brains, knock you out with drugs. I had a son . . ." He stopped. He paced again, out now into the silent, barren periphery of the room beyond, his tread heavy and rapid on the creaking floor. He walked to the leather couch and back again. When he spoke, his voice was somber and composed. "No, the more I think about it, Fenton, the more I feel we have no right to keep you, much as I would like to. In fact, I think it would be a good idea if you'd leave the country for a while. Could you arrange a couple of weeks' vacation, in Jamaica, for instance, at our expense . . . ?"

"Have you the authority to let me stay on the case?"

"I have, but I am morally and practically opposed. The risk's too great."

"Have I a voice in this? Would it be possible for *me* to overrule you, General?" The doctor smiled. And now he rose. He was as tall a man as the General, and their two giant shadows made restless colloquy on the opposite wall. "If you will tell me that, and I think you *want* to tell me that, sir, then I will gladly stay."

"The setup here would have to be completely changed," the General said musingly. "And your schedule. Some other base possibly. No." He spoke more firmly again, but with the same marked wistfulness. "You have no ax to grind in this. You are a civilian doing us a favor. Your life is worth as much as—well—his." He gestured toward the shadowy screen.

"Scarcely," said the doctor, also looking at it.

"*We* do not regard you as expendable. You have a practice."

"But little else," said Dr. Fenton.

The General peered at him over the rimless glasses.

"I am not married," the doctor said. He stared at the fire, feeling averse to the drama, the sentiment, the necessity of making a spectacle of himself, but realizing perhaps it was the only way. "I suppose you have wondered about that, General," he said awkwardly. "Possibly thought me a Don Juan or . . . worse. But the fact is . . .

"The fact is," he went on, listening to the roaring draft in the chimney above, and tilting his chin upward, "my major reason for living ended about twenty years ago—when my interest in psychiatry began. I don't make myself clear." He turned, taking out a cigarette. For this was hard to say. Nor might he have said it if this room had not been dim, the General a man that he respected, and this story possibly a straw.

"There was a girl, General. A very wonderful girl—whom

I knew in college. She was a talented pianist. She—went insane during one spring vacation. When I came back to Oberlin, she didn't show up. Her mother was a Dane—and a peculiar woman. She never told me where Kristin was. I had to find out all the details from the neighbors. But in all the years I've never been able to find that insane asylum . . ."

The General had sat down quietly.

"Her mother's dead now . . ." The doctor paused. He also took a chair, reached for a brandy glass. "So that may be one of the reasons I'm psychologically ripe for this thing. I don't want to give it up. And I certainly don't have as great a stake in living as, say, a man with a wife and kids." He gulped the brandy. "And aside from personal reasons, I'd hate to think that I wasn't a match for these bastards. I'd also hate to see the best brain in the country in any other psychiatrist's hands. It's—egotism, too." He smiled at last across the braided rug.

"And patriotism, too, I'd say." The General rose. He ambled to the pie-crust table, picked up a lump of sugar, crumbled it. "Well . . ." He seemed to count each chimney brick. "I can only say that we will do our best to keep those people . . ."

Dr. Fenton smiled broadly. The General extended his hand. The doctor gripped it, though the occasion probably demanded some sort of a salute.

They talked after that about the patient and the future. The General felt that it was expedient to move the patient from Base X as soon as possible. But this would take arranging. Some new, even more secret installation must be found. Since this would take time and conferences, he suggested that the sessions be canceled for the time being. None would take place Friday, anyway.

"Stevens will notify you."

Meanwhile, the doctor was to walk cautiously, stay in as much as possible at night, and listen to no strangers. His schedule would probably be changed, and from now on he would leave from Idlewild.

And there it rested, over another brandy for the road—a road which after tonight might never be the same.

FOURTEEN

November 17 was Louisa's sixtieth birthday, and Dr. Fenton had suggested some weeks earlier that she celebrate by giving a dinner for some of her friends in the neighborhood. Louisa had been overwhelmed, at first with gruff gratitude, then, as the time neared, with self-importance.

The doctor's presence was an unsettled point right up to the very hour. He had been hesitant to ask if he might attend. There was a strong possibility that he might be on one of his nocturnal missions; and beyond that, Louisa might not even want him. She might fear his presence would put a damper on the party.

The doctor got home from the office about five-thirty. A surprised Louisa came bustling in from the kitchen. "You home?" she asked. "You're not going out tonight?"

"I thought I might catch a movie."

"Movie?" She hesitated. "Would you—"

"Do you want me?" He grinned.

"Of course," she said gruffly. "You gotta eat *some* where, ain't you?"

At seven, he sat in the basement dining room, presiding at a candlelit table. He sat at the head, Louisa at the foot, and between them assorted maids, baby-sitters and the local butcher, all dressed to the nines. At first stiff and self-conscious, they had loosened up fast under the influence of the champagne he had provided, and were now gobbling their turkey dinner with an enthusiasm that bordered on avarice.

87

"Gravy?" the doctor asked the lady on his right, an elderly lady in blue lace who by day took care of newborn infants.

Shaking her head, she continued her diatribe. "Them mothers! Doctor, I'm telling you, you leave them alone and they'd kill the poor little things."

He nodded sympathetically, reflecting that he would prefer to be talking to the butcher, a jovial, portly man with an encyclopedic knowledge of sports, politics and women.

Upstairs the front doorbell rang.

"I'll get it, Doctor." Handsome in black taffeta, Louisa was giggling at something the butcher had just said.

"Not on your birthday." The doctor bowed to the lady in blue lace. "Will you keep an eye on those two for me, please?"

The laughter followed him upstairs.

At that moment, warmed by the champagne and by the good feeling downstairs, the doctor had no thought of conspirators. The past weeks, ever since his talk with the General, had been quiet. No more letters from Green. No telephone calls, except one from Stevens to cancel the sessions until further notice. The reason given was that there had been a small fire at Base X, quickly controlled, nothing serious.

The bell rang again as the doctor approached the door.

He opened it. Standing there was a slim, dark girl, dressed in black.

It was the girl he had seen at the Astor.

"Dr. Fenton . . ."

"Yes?"

"Could I see you for a few minutes, please, Doctor?"

He looked across the street, then left and right. The night was raw, one of those veiled November nights when the street lamps wear an aureole and cars slip by like shadows. Mist drifted over the sidewalks.

"Doctor," she said, and the beautiful eyes were pleading. "I am Angela Mallory."

She returned his gaze timidly, but unwaveringly. "Come in," he said, finally.

The parrot was in the parlor, its cage ornamented with ribbons for the occasion. He was standing on his trapeze, ripping up some tissue paper from one of Louisa's presents.

The girl did not even notice him. She turned, facing Dr. Fenton, wringing one black glove from her hand. Her flawless face was pale. The dark hair was half covered with a black scarf. Her flowing coat was of black velvet.

That it was the girl of the Astor he had no doubt. But was it the girl he had seen at the funeral? Her face had been covered that day. He had had an impression of veiled beauty. He could not be certain.

From the party below came whoops of laughter.

"I am extremely sorry to burst in on you this way," the girl said. She had no trace of accent. He tried to remember the voice he had heard over the Brooklyn telephone. That, as he recalled it, had been a voice like music, and this, too, charmed his ears.

He smiled ruefully. "You put me in a very difficult position, Mrs. Mallory," he said. "That is, if I can assume that you *are* Mrs. Mallory."

"Doctor"—her eyes widened, pleading—"I *swear* to you that I am."

"*Doctor!*" the parrot squawked, in a close imitation of the voice Louisa used in calling him to the telephone.

Taking notice of the bird for the first time, the girl smiled.

"Will you have a seat?" the doctor said.

"Thank you, sir." With the grace he'd noticed before, she dipped into a chair, then sat with expectant primness.

He went to the head of the stairway. "Louisa," he called. "Have your dessert without me. I'm very sorry, but I'll be delayed for a few minutes."

He returned to the parlor. The girl sat in half-profile, and again he felt a stab of wonderment at her beauty, a classic Renaissance face. The scarf had slipped back from the gleaming jet-black hair from which a few soft tendrils had been loosened. On one hand was a wedding ring.

89

He stood with his back to the mantel. "All right," he said. "Let's assume you *are* Mrs. Mallory. I have made a solemn promise to the government of the United States not to speak with you or anybody else. Strictly speaking it's my duty to ask you to leave."

Color flooded the pale cheeks, and he could not tell whether it was from anger or embarrassment. She rose, dropping one of the black gloves. "Doctor . . ." She moved toward him, and he could scent a fragrance like fresh violets. The big brown eyes were moist. "I *know* about these rules of silence. I have been asked to respect them too. And I *have* respected them. Even the other night at the Astor . . ."

He grunted.

"I apologize for doing that to you, sir. I—simply got cold feet. I sat there, trying to work up the courage to put the flower on, and I kept telling myself this is wrong. This is against the rules. You promised the General to keep quiet, and you are breaking that promise, and the General surely knows best."

Her voice was well bred and beautifully modulated. Some acting background?

"Undoubtedly he does know best," the doctor said. "And I was wrong myself to have gone against him."

"I should have spoken to you, then. I wish I had . . . but I am easily frightened." She rose, looking alternately flustered, pleading, and now, irresistibly childlike. "I put you to all that trouble, probably upset you, but if you will please forgive me, I will try to act better now. I want to help my husband get well, and that is all that matters to me . . ."

The parrot had come down off his trapeze, and now hung upside down from the bars, watching her with his bright shoe-button eyes.

"Hello, darling," the parrot said.

She turned, delighted. "How wonderful," she said.

"Just so you don't get any false impressions," the doctor

said, smiling, "it's something my housekeeper taught him. It's what she calls *him*."

"Oh, I see." Smiling in return, she perched on a sofa arm. When she smiled, dimples showed in each cheek. The dimples were a surprise against the stark dignity of her clothing, the ladylike coiffure, the serene face. He sensed depths of gaiety.

With that look she made him feel quite young.

"Doctor!" Louisa called from the stairway. "Your ice cream is melting right down to a puddle."

This bon mot evoked another gale of laughter from below.

"Right down to a puddle," repeated Louisa, heady with success.

"Will you excuse me a second, please?" the doctor said. He walked slowly down the stairs. He had found it hard to tear himself away. What to believe? There was *Who's Who*, the name given him by the fake Fitzgerald, and the little boy at the funeral. So many factors matched. And yet it was her effect upon himself which impressed him most. This woman could bemuse and capture men . . . a great scientist, a marine lieutenant . . . how many more?

The spotlight downstairs was on the butcher now, who had finally put on his funny paper hat, after vowing from the outset that he would not.

"I'm sorry, ladies and gentlemen," the doctor said. "There's a lady upstairs collecting for an orphanage. I won't be much longer."

"Don't let her hoodwink you," said the butcher sagely. "The woods are full of phonies."

"Shame on you," said the lady in blue lace. "Them orphans has to be taken care of some way."

"Dr. Fenton wouldn't even turn a sick cat away," said Louisa.

When the doctor returned to the parlor, his visitor was standing facing the hall door. She had removed her coat. The black silk dress was simple, modest. But there was elegance and taste in that simplicity. She was exquisitely built. She knew how to stand. She knew how to walk—not timidly now, but with the litheness of an animal.

"I won't take long, sir." Her brown eyes flashed. "I am sorry to seem so bold and rude, but I am going to stay until I tell you. Something very frightening happened to me last week. Doctor, you must listen."

"Mrs. Mallory," he said, "you have ways, I am sure, of communicating with the General. Don't you think it would be wiser . . . ?"

"I have no way of communicating with the General," she said, "except when he sees fit to call me. And he has not called me for two weeks."

"Then possibly I could arrange—"

"No." She stamped her foot. Color again mounted in her cheeks. "I want to tell *you*. You are my husband's doctor, and you are here, and I am here." She took a step toward him, and then drew back. "A man, a certain man came to see me the day after the funeral, my mother's funeral. My mother died recently. That is why I came to Brooklyn." Her voice was breathless, but determined. "This man came to see me. It was the same man . . ." She broke off, fluttering the long dark lashes. "To have it make any sense to you, I must begin from the beginning."

"Very well," Dr. Fenton muttered, annoyed to find his voice so hoarse. He moved to the coffee table, groping for a cigarette. What else, he thought? Pick her up bodily, and throw her out of the house?

"About a year ago," she said, "my husband made a trip for the government out west. It was our wedding anniversary a few days later, and he called me up. He asked me to fly out and meet him, so I did. His work was over, and he had rented a car. He picked me up at the airport, and then we drove to a big motel. We spent two days there, resting and doing some sightseeing. At this motel we met a man."

"Do you recall the name of this motel?"

"I don't recall the name of the motel, but I remember the

town," she said. She smiled wistfully. "One usually remembers places, Doctor, where things were fun. We had a wonderful two days . . . the last good time I can remember."

"The town?"

"Wichita Falls, Texas. We went swimming. It was more than a year ago, still summer. This motel had a swimming pool. My husband seemed so relaxed. It was like a honeymoon. I had left Johnny with my mother. Then—this man introduced himself."

The doctor walked to the coffee table. "Why don't you sit down?"

She sat near the parrot's cage, her eyes unwavering, very earnest. "I am only telling you all these details, Doctor, because they *all* seem so important now. This man . . . well, we were just sitting there beside the pool. He said that he had heard about my husband's work in Princeton. He said he himself was an Australian scientist, here in this country on a fellowship. He was very gentlemanly, very nice, very interesting."

"Oh *yes!*" the parrot said.

She took no notice. "I went inside after a while, to dress, and left them alone." She smiled a fleeting smile. "Actually, Doctor, scientific shoptalk is still way over my head. When I came out, they were still talking—and my husband had invited the man to have dinner with us. I've never seen him so intrigued with anyone. You know, ordinarily, he is not sociable. But after dinner, they went for a ride, and were gone for *hours* . . ."

Her voice shook slightly. She rose from her chair, turned toward the door and seemed to listen for a second. When she turned to him, her face was paler.

"Doctor, that same man, that stranger, showed up in Brooklyn at my mother's house. He came to see me. He said that he had read my mother's obituary in the papers, and that he had come to offer sympathy. But why? He scarcely knew me. And I *knew* he was only there to snoop. About my husband.

Because that was all he talked about. He seemed to know, somehow, God knows how, that my husband was out of his mind." She spoke more breathlessly. "He stayed and stayed. I couldn't get rid of him. He kept asking questions. And my brother came home. Johnny was there. He found out far too much!"

The dark head lowered.

"What did he find out?" She did not answer. "What did he look like," asked the doctor.

"Oh, he *looks* respectable." She looked up nervously. "Quite nice-looking, and with a sort of English accent. His hair was cut short, blond, a little taller than me" (she looked about five feet five) "and I could never guess his age. His face looked old—older than his body."

"What was his name?"

"Mr. Reginald Arbuthnot . . . But—that isn't all, Doctor." She twisted her slender hands, moving between the highboy and the mantel. "After he was gone, I called the fellowship fund he'd mentioned. They'd never heard of any Mr. Arbuthnot . . ."

Fitzgerald—Arbuthnot?

"This, Mrs. Mallory," Dr. Fenton said, "is certainly something to report to the General."

"I will, I will if he ever calls me," she said. "Though he will be very angry. I managed things so poorly. But I was taken by surprise. I hesitate—"

"Of course," the doctor murmured. He picked up her coat. "I'll be happy to pave the way."

"My story isn't finished, Doctor." She was standing directly beneath his father's portrait now, more desperation in the beautiful face. Her lips were trembling. "I am guilty on another score. And this may be important to *you*. It is really the reason I have come. Have you a moment more?"

He was sure, considering the sounds below, that the feast had reached satiety. "Games" and after-dinner drinks were next on the agenda. But he smiled and laid her coat and scarf aside.

"I have thought of it before," she said, "but I did not realize the connection until Mr. Arbuthnot came back. But I *do* think meeting him changed our life for us. My husband was a different person after Wichita Falls. He certainly wasn't as affectionate, and that was when his headaches started. He had a vile headache the very next day. And—well, I had the feeling something was hanging over him."

"What?" the doctor asked.

"I couldn't tell. I don't know what they talked about. I didn't *connect* the change with Mr. Arbuthnot," she answered. "In fact"—she smiled ruefully—"all my married life I have made allowances for Dr. Mallory's moods. He is not an ordinary person, Doctor." She seemed for the first time to become aware of the sounds from below, the scraping of chairs, the tramp of feet. Hastily she reached for the coat and scarf. "Now I have told you. Now it's off my conscience."

"Very interesting," the doctor murmured.

Very, *very* interesting.

He was tempted to keep her there and question her more closely. But she now seemed as determined to leave as she had been to stay. Tossing the scarf about her hair, she glided out into the hall.

"Thank you very much," she said. "And if you want to, you can tell the General."

"How did you get my name? Through Mr. Arbuthnot?"

"No. Oh no." Dimpling, she tied the scarf beneath her chin. "From the General."

"The General?"

"Well, not *directly* from him. But he said that the greatest authority on genius in New York was treating my husband. So I called up two different hospitals, and they both said Dr. Fenton. I've also read your book."

She turned the doorknob.

"I thought it was just marvelous." The fog, the cold rolled

in. "Thank you for listening to me." She poised for a second on the high stone stoop. "And I hope you will forgive me . . ."

"Good night, Mrs. Mallory." He watched her swift flight down the steps, her disappearance into the fog.

He turned, surprised to find Louisa at his elbow.

"Hmph!" Louisa said.

"What does that mean exactly, Louisa?"

"Hmph!" she repeated.

FIFTEEN

"Congratulations, Doctor!" He heard the General's voice even as Stevens was removing the blindfold. The General was stretching out a hand, a smile on his face. Also smiling were Dr. Throckmorton and Major Brown, who had followed the General in. "I think you've done it. What? Didn't Stevens tell you?"

Stevens had told the doctor nothing. They had met at Idlewild. Dr. Fenton had known it was going to be the same Base X only when they had skimmed over the familiar concrete highway, crossed the rumbling bridge and hit the pine woods. They had sat on that plane for an hour and a half like mummies.

"Well"—the General smiled at Stevens—"perhaps he wanted *me* to have the pleasure." He patted Stevens' shoulder. "A good man, Doctor. Emotional discipline here. A perfectionist . . . But sit down. We won't need any fire this evening. Warm enough *within*." He touched his chest. His step was springy, and, surrounded by his cohorts, he appeared as happy as a king who is about to announce the birth of a son and heir.

"What's happened, sir?" The doctor followed him to the leather couch. The wing chairs and the pie-crust table had been removed, and the room returned again to its former drab appearance.

The General bestowed a benevolent smile on the opposite end of the room.

The doctor followed his glance. It was resting on the screen.

"Doctor, the patient has drastically, immeasurably improved. He makes sense. He has snapped back to normal."

The doctor turned instinctively to Dr. Throckmorton, who was standing with flushed cheeks beside the General's couch. Dr. Throckmorton nodded, his blue eyes bright.

"Just when we were at our lowest point," the General said. And he leaned forward, heaving a happy sigh and smoothing his well-creased trousers. "Do you remember our last talk, when we both felt very low about the future? I felt —well, probably lower than you." He looked around, sat back. "These men deserved some sort of break. Winter, this colder weather, worried me. You know, our transportation and supply facilities could be ruined by a heavy snow. *Your* information worried me." Still looking pleased, he said, "I had the feeling, though I *was* encouraged by your progress, that our man's illness might stretch on indefinitely. And—where was I to find a base of operations as excellent as this? I knew it might prove bad psychology for him to be moved, as well as our having to face the cost and practical difficulties of such an operation, which would have to be accomplished quickly and with a minimum of publicity."

The General, unfortunately, was a wordy man. He liked tangents and preambles. The doctor stirred under this barrage, his eyes impatiently moving toward the screen.

But the story had to be recounted in every detail.

To add to his troubles, the General said, his own foolishness or selfishness (not the staff's fault, certainly) had caused an accident. He never should have lit a fire in that old chimney. After his departure from Base X that very night, sparks which must have drifted unnoticed into the woods nearby and smoldered there among the underbrush had broken into a full-scale blaze. The neighboring trees had gone up in flames, an alarming thing, for the wind had freshened. It was close to dawn. Billowing clouds of smoke had awakened the staff, and all hands had had to work their heads off to extinguish the blaze. For they could not, naturally, call up the rural fire department. And there had been the problem, too, that the glow against the sky might attract some farmer, or passing motorist. Fortunately it hadn't. Nor had the house itself been badly damaged. But it had seemed a close call, and an evil omen.

"However, what is that old adage?" The General was now on his feet, his sermon moving to a climax. "It is always darkest before the dawn? Or an ill wind always blows some good? Far from destroying our hopes, that night gave birth to them. Doctor"—he smiled—"I do not mean to storm your bailiwick. But I cannot help but believe, and, as a matter of fact, Dr. Throckmorton himself suggested it, that fear of his life, the presence of that fire, and the possibility that he might be burned alive like a horse trapped in a burning barn, might have turned the tide of his mind."

"Was he in danger?" Dr. Fenton asked.

"Only for the briefest period," said the General. "Dr. Throckmorton immediately went down and stayed beside his bed, giving him all the comfort necessary. Dr. Throckmorton naturally had a problem, whether to move him out of the house into the fresh air. The smoke had penetrated the sickroom, and the patient was coughing violently. He compromised by prying loose one of the boards covering the windows, and then he telephoned me."

The General turned to Dr. Throckmorton, bestowing another one of those broad smiles. "Poor Bill had quite a night of it. But, as I've said, Doctor, the place is intact. And the patient is not only none the worse for it, but it has wrought a change."

Dr. Fenton turned to Dr. Throckmorton, a pretty frail-looking old hero. "How did the patient react while you were with him?" he asked the immaculate old man.

"Oh, he was very frightened. He moaned and clung to me," said Dr. Throckmorton, glancing at the General. That night's experience seemed to have started a facial tic, for one cheek twitched as he repeated his last statement. "He moaned and clung to me. He kept saying he was afraid to die. He didn't want to die, and I should take him out of the house.

"I gave him a sedative," he went on. "The fire by that time was getting under control. Well, he slept for hours afterwards." He touched the twitching cheek. "In fact, for nearly a day. He was spared the sight of all the confusion afterwards. The board, you see, had to be hammered back, but he didn't even wake up when the Major hammered." He smiled. "I had given him a pretty strong dose. And by the time he woke, we'd cleared his room of smoke. I had changed his mask. He was fresh as a daisy, and we decided to tell him nothing about the fire. We hoped that it had passed from his mind in sleep."

"Had it?"

"Well, he hasn't referred to it at all again."

"What has he referred to?"

"Doctor—" Dr. Throckmorton began, his face embarrassed. "He has referred . . ." He paused, looking toward the General timidly, then back to Dr. Fenton. "I cannot describe it, or even understand it in *your* terms. What has occurred within his brain. But the man seems *well*. Utterly and completely like a normal individual."

"Since he woke from the sedative?"

"Not—exactly . . ." Dr. Throckmorton pursed his lips. "For a couple of days he lay—well, pretty much as he was when you first came here. Very silent, apathetic. Wearing his mask, of course, and only firing up when we came near it. But on Wednesday afternoon last week, he called for me. He asked Pete to bring me in, referring to me by my name. And he has never used it before, or regarded *me* as a friend. I went in.

He shook my hand politely. He asked me where he was. I told him. And—there was no speech difficulty."

"There has been not a trace since then," the General added. "He comes right out with everything. Voice is just as normal as yours and mine."

"Hmm," said Dr. Fenton. "What else?" to Dr. Throckmorton.

"Since then, he has been polite, sociable. He has eaten his meals, taken an interest in everything. And he has asked to leave."

"The microphones have picked up all this?"

"No. We have not had them on. Some of the wiring was destroyed, or rather it got wet from all the water and the chemicals."

Major Brown now spoke. "I am afraid your interview to-night will have to be live, Doctor. That is, through the screen without amplification. But his voice level is pretty good. It penetrates."

"Have *you* spoken much to him, sir?" Dr. Fenton asked the General.

"I have," answered the big man calmly, and with conviction. "Both in this room and out. I've been in and out of his room all day," he added, smiling, taking off his glasses and polishing them as he talked. "Making my *own* tests—because I couldn't, for many hours, accept the truth. But it's amazing!" Putting the glasses back on, he sighed, stood up—and by that gesture, subtle but commanding, seemed to dismiss his court, for the onlookers now began to edge toward the doors. "Prayer," he said, as though pronouncing a benediction on them all. "Prayer is an amazing thing. Doctor, I do not know whether you are a religious man, or what your theories are about the power of faith. But to me, this seems a proof that God does listen."

His voice shook slightly. He was very sincere and his audience very solemn. But what the devil! Schizophrenics did not turn overnight into "well" men, no matter how many worthy generals went down on their knees.

"I cannot wait until you hear him for yourself," the General said. "And may I have your permission to remain?" He nodded toward the retreating staff, who would, now that there was no monitor, perhaps remain in the corridor at the keyhole, or even in the patient's room. "I would like to see your face," he added.

"Certainly, sir."

He sat down at his desk.

The General stood at a distance, near the center of the room, his hands behind his back. The doctor pressed the signal button, but it seemed to be out of order. So did the mechanism which controlled the doors. It was soon obvious that they were being opened manually.

He could hear footsteps and faint whispering. He cleared his throat. All was perfectly quiet now.

"Good evening. I am Dr. Fenton," he began.

No answer. The General tiptoed forward.

"Make it a little louder, perhaps?" How anxious, earnest his face was. He was perspiring.

"Good evening. I am Dr. Fenton."

"Fenton?" came a baritone voice. Rather deeper than the one he'd known, though he had not heard it for a while. It was muffled by the canvas.

"Yes . . ."

"Good evening, Dr. Fenton. How are you?"

Still off in the distance somewhere, rather stiff—but to do the General justice, the voice of a sane man.

"How are *you?*"

"Me? I'm just fine!"

SIXTEEN

"I'm okay, all straightened out now," he said in the same muffled tones. The doctor missed the amplifiers. He had grown used to hearing every change in tone quality, catching all the nuances. The screen must not only be acting as a deadening agent, it also gave the voice a distorted quality.

"I'm all right. I don't need any treatment."

He was not, certainly, any abject, clinging personality tonight. Quite guarded, a trifle hostile, and, in spite of the General's remarks, not too co-operative, at first. But he seemed willing to answer questions.

"Where are you?"

"In a mental hospital—of sorts." He laughed.

"Do you know your name?"

"Yes. Eric Mallory."

Dr. Fenton looked instinctively at the General. But the latter was smiling blandly. It was as though he felt no further need for secrecy.

"How old are you?"

"Thirty-eight."

"Do you remember your date of birth?"

"What?"

"What's your birthday, the day you were born?"

"July 29, 1920."

"What work do you do?"

"I am an atomic physicist."

The patient was imperceptibly relaxing, though his voice still sounded strained—and strange. Odd how mechanics could deceive one. He had not thought the timbre quite so resonant.

Or was this merely the effect of a clearing brain?

In any case, there had been so far no effort in enunciating the sentences. No trace of gagging, gasping. The answers came without a moment's hesitation.

"Are you married, sir?"

"Yes, I am."

"What is your wife's name?"

"Angela Romagna Mallory."

"How old is your wife?"

"Twenty-seven and a half." More pleasantly he said. "And *her* birthday is the twenty-eighth of March."

"Have you any children?"

"One. A boy."

"How old?"

"Four and a half. His name is John."

It was open house on secrets tonight for a fact. The General, posed as for a sculptor, stayed in that one spot, his head erect, taking in everything, not looking at the doctor at all, just waiting for the next words, a man humble before the power of a miracle.

And miracle it seemed.

For, in rather grudging fashion, but always perfectly informed, the patient now proved that he was well oriented and had an intact memory. He knew the names of all the staff, the General's name and the General's position. He recited past historical events and dates, the names of the presidents, all the determinants used in elemental psychology. He did not once strike out.

The doctor then threw a few curves, questions that crosschecked other questions, and even questions that carried a sting. These the patient met with aplomb, and occasionally a slight chuckle. Since a sense of humor was usually absent in the psychotic, this was encouraging. Obviously he was feeling more at ease.

By now the General was walking up and down in high excitement, pleased as punch. He walked up to the doctor, and spoke in a whisper. "Try him on loyalty . . ."

"What is your opinion of the United States?" asked Dr. Fenton.

"I am a citizen of the United States."

"I asked you for your opinion of the United States."

"I have a lot of opinions about the United States."

"Favorable or unfavorable?"

The General drew in a deep and audible breath. He held it.

"I don't like supermarkets, Hollywood starlets, traffic circles, or Lawrence Welk." He laughed. So did the General.

"How about the government?"

"The government's—fine."

"You admire the present government?"

"I do," he said, with utter calm.

"What are your political affiliations?"

"How do I vote? Republican or Democrat?"

"Yes."

It was more like a court trial now—with the General presiding as judge, and Dr. Fenton, the prosecuting attorney— than the examination of a sick man.

"I do not vote. I am not interested in politics."

"Are you a Communist?"

"Most certainly not."

Gone were all the vagueness, suffering, confusion and fear —most definitely. His panic seemed to have vanished with those microphones.

"Do you admire the scientific program of the United States?"

"I certainly do. It's wonderful."

Strong emphasis, and even surprise, as though it were unthinkable he should be asked.

"In relation to other countries' scientific programs?"

"We're smarter than the Russians, the Germans, and certainly the English, if that is what you mean."

"Do you find fault with any aspects of your particular job?"

"Absolutely not."

"May I read you one of your former statements?" the doctor asked quietly. He ran through his notebook, put on his glasses and recited the patient's secretary's testimony. She had heard the patient threaten to blow up the laboratory.

"This was said by you on the afternoon you were taken ill. Do you remember saying it?"

"No, sir."

"You deny its pertinence to yourself?"

"I do not understand the question."

"Is the statement real? Does it express what you secretly have always felt, do feel?"

"No, sir."

"You renounce this statement?"

"Yes. I do not recall ever having made it," said the patient. And now, with certain noises, as though he had clambered from his bed to the floor and walked, unmolested, closer to the screen, he "explained" his illness.

He explained it as a form of mental blackout. Amnesia, if he could employ one of the doctor's terms. He was very self-confident by this time, and the voice was stronger, more effusive and intense. During that period, from late September to last Wednesday, "something had happened" to him, which he could only explain as possibly physical, the result of a blow.

There had been no "blows," the doctor answered. No neurological evidence of concussion. Did the patient recall having been struck by anybody?

"No. It's as you say, Doctor. But I *do* know when I woke that morning, my head ached badly. Migraine. I am subject to them. Could migraine cause amnesia?"

"I doubt it, but describe your symptoms."

"Well, I had this headache, but I went to work. I can remember that morning very clearly. Everything looked far *brighter* than usual. The color of my wife's dress, for example. It was lavender. And our boy wore a yellow T-shirt.

When I got into my car, its color seemed almost blinding. My car is blue, a Buick, robin's-egg blue."

He waited, as though for a word of approbation. Certainly, if the General had been the interviewer, one would have come. That stalwart gentleman had never looked more entranced. His lips hung slack, his hands hung limp, his eyebrows jutted forward.

"Go on, please."

"By two o'clock things were so bright as to be unbearable. And my head felt twice its size. The pain was excruciating. I thought of going home, and was about to, when suddenly everything seemed to snap. Stars flashed. I couldn't see any more, and"—he paused, heaved in a sigh—"and the next thing I was here."

"That's all?" asked Dr. Fenton.

"That's all, sir. Positively."

"You don't remember striking anybody?"

"No. Did I strike anybody?"

"Tearing papers up?"

"Papers? My own *work*. No, sir. Nothing until I came to last Wednesday. And believe me, sir, *that* was a shock." He waited, chuckled, and again he waited, stirring restlessly.

"You may lie down again," said Dr. Fenton. For he knew the man was at the screen. He could see the bulges that his face, perhaps his hands, were making in its canvas surface. "Don't tire yourself. That will be all for now. Thank you, Dr. Mallory. Good night."

"All for *now!*" cried the strained voice. The bulges on the canvas moved. "I'm *well*. Good God, man. I want to *leave*. I don't need any treatments."

"You may be right. However . . ."

"I want my wife. I want to work." Aggrieved, almost frantic. "Are you going to punish me for a little headache? Give me a prescription . . ." The hands pressed violently.

The General hurried out.

"I've given you enough proof!"

The bulges disappeared. Smothered muttering and shuffling, the padding of tennis shoes. Then somebody, perhaps the patient, cursed. He heard a grunt. There was loud creaking, the sound of metal. And finally the doors slammed shut.

Was it a miracle?

"Amnesia" was too cheap a theory.

Those tests had barely scratched the surface.

In the hubbub of discussion which followed (and hope flowed as copiously as the Scotch) the doctor almost forgot to hand in his report on Mrs. Mallory to the General. She, who had seemed so important an item five hours ago, had now sunk to a postscript, but he remembered her at last and turned in the facts about her visit, which he had scribbled down on the plane.

The General read them cursorily. His face was still pink with optimism.

"I think," said the doctor, when the General had finished reading, "that we have every reason to believe that the man who visited her was the same one who came to see me, in spite of the difference in names."

"It would appear that way," said the General. He pocketed the doctor's notes. "I think maybe we'll have a line on the gentleman before too very long. In any case, I think that, whatever he may be up to, he's a little late." He brightened. "A headstrong little strumpet, isn't she?" He laughed heartily. "I guess you can see now why the patient might be in a hurry to get back to bedside, can't you?"

"A very attractive woman." The doctor paused. "Do I understand, then, General, that you no longer feel there's any great risk involved in my having seen her?"

"Well, I'd say we're out of the woods now, wouldn't you, Doctor?" The General earnestly sipped his drink.

"It would certainly appear so on the surface," the doctor said. "Of course, *her* testimony . . ." He stopped. Looking at the screen, he said, "This may be temporary. He may revert."

"Of course," said the General genially. "I've considered that. I don't want to be in a hurry and have to backtrack. Naturally not. What do you think? He showed a *little* temper. Another session or two, to make sure it's not merely an, uh . . ."

"At the very least," the doctor said.

The General nodded. "Two, I should think, would be enough."

The doctor drained his glass.

"General, do I have your permission to talk with Mrs. Mallory?"

"Do you feel it's important?"

"I want to be absolutely convinced in my own mind about the patient's recovery. I would like to do a little following-up on this Wichita Falls business. And I'm sure that she'd be very interested to hear about his improvement."

"Oh, of course," the General said. "We'll be notifying her, naturally, although I don't want to raise her hopes prematurely. But . . . Fenton . . ." The General's eyes twinkled.

"Yes?"

"I've heard it said that a psychiatrist worthy of his salt never really discharges a patient. Once he grabs hold, he never lets go. That's not true in your case, is it?" The General grinned expansively at his own joke.

Dr. Fenton forced a hollow laugh. "We're unduly maligned," he said.

SEVENTEEN

Pigeons fluttered from the low red roofs, wheeling off against a cold blue sky. The sound of their wings was loud and distinct, for a moment the only sound on the block. The neighborhood was hushed and still on this wintry Sunday afternoon. Far down the street he saw a little girl twirling a hulahoop. Smoke curled from a chimney. The pigeons flew up against the cold sun, banked in unison, and came winging back.

The Romagna house looked bleak. The glassed-in porch was bare, and the curtains down upstairs. A "For Sale" sign leaned askew in the small front yard.

He was ten minutes earlier than he had said he would be when he telephoned, but when he touched the bell, the door opened instantly, as if she had been watching for him. She crossed the empty porch, dressed in a black skirt, white blouse and dark cardigan. "How very kind of you, Doctor." Her face was flushed. "Please come in."

Behind the porch was a somber parlor hung with heavy brown portieres.

"This is Johnny," she said. A little boy had scrambled up from the floor. "Doctor, I should like you to meet my son. Johnny, this nice man is Dr. Fenton." It was the child he had seen with her at the funeral. Today he was in dungarees and yellow T-shirt.

The doctor held out his hand, but the boy did not take it. He hid behind his mother. His hair was light brown and his eyes dark brown. Though pale, he was a good-looking little boy.

The doctor smiled. "Hi, Johnny."

Finally the boy gave a timid smile and took the doctor's hand. Then he turned shyly away. He leaned against a sofa.

"Let's see if Uncle Victor wants to play a game of checkers." Very gently she coaxed him back behind the brown portieres. "Please make yourself at home, Doctor."

It was the sort of house he remembered from early boyhood, like his grandmother's house. Old world, old-fashioned, with heavy scrolled furniture, stained woodwork, lace antimacassars, and enough family photographs to fill a gallery. The only modern touch was a huge console television set.

109

He scanned the photographs. The Romagna men struck very dramatic poses. There were stiff little girls in white dresses, first-communion pictures, no doubt. And many bridal groups. He saw none which included a man with light brown hair and glasses. But he was examining one, when she returned. It was indubitably Angela, dressed in medieval costume and with her long black hair hanging down her shoulders.

She carried a tray with a decanter and two glasses. Catching him near the photograph, she laughed. "That's me in high school. I played Juliet. And I was terrible."

"Were you an actress, Mrs. Mallory?"

"Before my marriage? No. I wanted to be. I went a year to dramatic school. But I ended up modeling fur coats in A and S's." She set the tray on a table topped with dark blue glass. Where had she acquired that air of aristocracy? "Or would you have preferred coffee, Doctor?"

"No, thank you. I drink too much coffee." So far she had not mentioned her husband, and he wondered if the General had telephoned. "This is certainly much better hospitality than I offered you," he said.

"It is my mother's wine," she said. "She made it every year, including *this* year." She smiled a gentle smile. Then she sighed. "Doctor, the General called this morning. Is it true? Is my husband cured?"

He did not speak for a moment. "Your husband has undergone a change, a very remarkable one in the past week. He speaks intelligently, and has renounced his threats," he answered carefully.

Her eyes gazed into his.

"But, Mrs. Mallory, it is a trifle early to say that he is cured. Didn't the General tell you that?"

"Oh yes, but he was so enthusiastic." She picked up her glass. Then she looked toward the brown portieres. From beyond came a heavy creaking step. In a lower voice, she said, "It would naturally affect my plans. I cannot stay on here."

"I noticed the For Sale sign," the doctor said.

"Yes, but it is already sold. We sold it yesterday." She sighed. "My brother Victor was the only one who lived with Mama, and he is leaving Brooklyn. He—" She rose. "Excuse me." Raising her voice she called, "How is the checker game going?"

A man's voice answered in Italian.

"Excuse me." She disappeared through the portieres, and soon came back. When she sat down again, her tone was even softer. "Mainly I did not want Johnny to hear the plans. You see, we have a house to go to . . ." She smiled. "You like the wine?"

"Excellent," the doctor said.

She poured him another glass.

"You mean your husband's house?" the doctor asked.

"Yes. Though two of my sisters have been begging me to visit them." Still she spoke conspiratorially. "But if there is hope for my husband, I should be home. Don't you think so, Doctor?"

"Mrs. Mallory, as I've said before . . ."

"Anyway"—she turned her head uneasily—"as soon as I have helped Victor with the moving, I shall leave." She set her glass down firmly. "I must think only of what is best for Dr. Mallory . . ."

"Of course," he said.

"Have you been able to question him yet about Mr. Arbuthnot? I told the General all that I told you."

"I have only begun to scratch the surface of your husband's problems, Mrs. Mallory. Much remains to be done." The brown portieres swayed softly. Lowering his voice, he said, "I suppose you realize that Mr. Arbuthnot was not all he was cracked up to be."

"I meant has Dr. Mallory mentioned him?"

"No, but that place you mentioned, Wichita Falls . . ." He

stopped. Her eyes were dark, intent. All was expectancy, and yet the persistent illusion of someone eavesdropping, plus all the preservations of the old taboos seemed like iron bands. "Mrs. Mallory," he said, "it's wonderful to be able to talk with you, but would it be possible for us, say, to take a walk? Or do you have to stay?"

"No, let's go out," she said. And she got up so abruptly and so eagerly it was almost as though she herself had been hoping for his suggestion. "But it's so cold. You must be tired."

"Is it too cold for you?"

"I haven't been out of this house for days. Not to go anywhere. Except to *your* house—and the Hotel Astor." The dimples showing again, she vanished. Then from behind the brown portieres prompt altercation began in low Italian. Her voice was rapid, pleading. The man seemed angry and suspicious. When she returned, her cheeks were flushed.

She was dressed in the flowing coat, and round her head was a scarf of lavender. It added new dimension to her beauty, the violet hue enhanced the peachlike skin, the vivid eyes and the dark hair. She looked no older than eighteen.

The sun shone on the steeple of the church beyond, but its light was paler in this street. The pigeons had left the sky. They walked past the school, the church, their footsteps making the only sounds in this Sunday stillness, so different from that day in late October. Here the band had marched, and there, on those church steps, he had strained his eyes for a glimpse of this exquisite child.

How different she seemed now from that veiled mystery woman—swinging along like a schoolgirl, head held high, and talking eagerly. When they passed the church, however, she stopped talking, lowered her head and mutely crossed herself. She had begun talking almost from the moment they were out of the house, again on the subject of Mr. Arbuthnot and the effect the rendezvous at Wichita Falls had made on "Dr. Mallory." Strangely enough, he had not once heard her refer to her husband by his first name. "Dr. Mallory" had grown irritable, forgetful, and complained of headaches.

Once they were past the church and all its memories, she laughed apologetically.

"It's silly to talk about his being *more* forgetful. My husband was naturally absent-minded."

"In what particulars?" the doctor asked.

"Oh, many, many things. Like birthdays, wedding anniversaries . . ." She added loyally, "Not that he wouldn't stand on his head to make it up when he forgot. But before we went to Wichita Falls, I had to remind him it was our sixth anniversary." She stopped, then said with dignity, "But a genius does not need to remember little things."

"He seems less absent-minded now," the doctor said, remembering the sharp retorts from behind the screen. "Your birthday rolled right off the tip of his tongue."

"Good. That's *very* good." She nodded, pleased.

They passed an El, and he began to smell a mingled aroma of hot corn, hot dogs, hot knishes and salt air. They were on the outskirts of Coney Island. Most of the concession fronts were boarded up, but the Ferris wheel was turning, screams came from the roller coaster, and little children galloped round and round on ponies.

They stood before a wide, bright boulevard, swept with wind.

"What is he really like?" the doctor asked. He noticed that she was shivering. "Shall we turn back?"

"No." Her eyes were bright. "Dear old Coney Island. I love it. Let's go on." She breathed in deeply. "The air is wonderful.

"What was my husband like?" she asked when they had crossed toward Steeplechase. "That seems a funny question for you to ask me, Doctor. I should be asking you what he is like." She smiled, and said with deep respect, "You have such understanding."

The doctor smiled. "Not of your husband. Mrs. Mallory,"

he continued, as they strolled on against the wind toward the sea, "you may not know the circumstances under which I've treated him. They have not been helpful to a diagnosis. I have used my imagination," he said hastily, for she had paused as though in alarm. "And of course I've formed an impression of his character. But it may be wrong. His recent improvement has confused me."

"What was this impression?"

They mounted sandy steps, the boardwalk steps.

"Well, I have thought of him as dreamy, absent-minded, the way you just described him. The typical idealist, though 'typical' is a word I very much dislike." He breathed deeply. The wind seemed to be snatching the words away, and making them pedantic. The view and this deeply sensitive young woman demanded poetry, not pedantry.

Up here on the deserted promenade, late sunlight, cold and brilliant, gave wan color to the beach, struck dazzling highlights in the sea. And the ocean thundered, drew back, thundered.

"A man of genius," he almost had to shout. "A man like that—" He nodded out across the blue expanse. "As big as that—and as hard for a human being like me to comprehend." Yes, that had been his early impression of the sick man. But not all. He turned his back to the wind. "But you and jazz music added warmth to it. Color and youth. I knew that he was human . . ."

She stood before him, not responding to the smile. Her head was bowed. She shivered again.

"Are you frozen?"

"No." She lifted the small chin firmly. "Let's walk a little farther. This is very helpful . . ."

They were approaching a carrousel when she spoke again. He could hear its music above the steady roar of the breakers. The tune was "Roses from the South."

"I wish I could have understood my husband," she began. "I wish I could—well—have seen into his heart. But he was older . . ." She broke off, looking shyly up into his face. "Seven years may seem like a long marriage, Doctor. But I was very young when we were married."

"Twenty-one?" he asked.

"Not quite twenty-one," she said. "And who was I? I was modeling fur coats. I had a high-school education. I could not imagine what Dr. Mallory saw in me. He was so very brilliant. He was older. He had gone to college—and abroad —to famous universities. It was sort of—like, well, marrying Prince Rainier." She blushed and looked abashed before his smiling glance. "Not that I'm any Grace Kelly."

"Your husband has always spoken of you devotedly," he said.

"Yes, Dr. Mallory has been kind to me. He has been patient with me, never ashamed. He tried to educate me, he was faithful." She walked in silence, and now it was as though imperceptibly she was keeping time to the wheezy waltz music. She paused before the carrousel. "He was a *good* man, Doctor, very good. He let me keep my own religion, he bought me clothes. I was a lucky woman, Doctor."

"He was a lucky man."

"Yes . . . Maybe so . . ." Now she was turning suddenly, shivering again, sweeping the long coat in an arc. "Shall we go back now, Doctor?"

He strode beside her, mystified and troubled. The light was paler and less brilliant now. All color was gone from the sea beyond. The vast expanse looked lifeless, leaden.

"Doctor, there is something, though, that I would like to ask you."

"Ask away."

"I am not too familiar with psychiatry. I read *your* book— and some others since my husband was taken ill. It's—about Johnny. He sometimes worries me."

"How so?"

It was quite a while before she answered. "Johnny loves his father very much," she said, with care. "I am certain of

115

that. And his father is very crazy about Johnny. He loves him very dearly. I'm sure that he does. But, as you say, his father is a dreamer—and a marvelous genius," she falteringly went on. "He cannot be expected to be a husband and a father like other fathers, can he?"

"I should imagine there are many different forms of father-hood, all of which include being a *good* father," he said lamely.

"You are not a father, Dr. Fenton?"

"No," he said. "I have never married."

"Oh, how perfectly beautiful!" she said breathlessly, and stopped walking. The lights along the boulevard had just come on. "Don't they look pretty?"

He agreed. And yet the impulsive reaction, the timing of it had given him a start. In fact, annoyingly, he had experienced a thrill. He was furious at himself.

They left the line of lights, stepped down into rapidly darkening streets, and began to retrace the route by which they had come.

"Johnny," she picked up the conversation again beyond the boulevard, "doesn't seem to want to go home at all. And he has asthma there."

"You have had treatment for him?"

"Yes. They tell me it is all nerves." She looked up anxiously. "I do not mean to imply, Doctor, that it is his father's fault. I spoil him. I was brought up to spoil children, love them half to death. But boys, I guess, should not have spoiling mothers. At least the books say that. But—" She fell silent once again.

"But what?"

"You see, I felt that I alone cannot make him into a man, or bring him up like other boys. He needs companionship, and to *know* his father. So would it be too much to ask you, when you begin the therapy, could you put in some little word for Johnny? I feel sure that Dr. Mallory would listen to you."

"I certainly shall. I shall try," he said.

"Thank you." After this, she seemed to brighten. Looking up at him, her eyes were grateful. "I think it's wonderful the General found you. I feel so much confidence in your ability, Doctor. You know"—her voice rose blithely—"the General said something today—that an ill wind blows somebody some good. And when I went to Mass, I thought about it. Yes. Maybe my husband's illness was—from God. Maybe he will come out of it a better person." She took a skipping step.

"Am I walking too fast for you?"

"No. Oh no."

"How about a cab?"

"I like to walk. Do you think a nervous breakdown can change a person, Doctor? Once they are over it?"

He smiled awkwardly, looking down into the sweet and trusting face. It was as transparent as a brook, and just as soothing to a troubled man. Was that the secret of her ineffable charm? Transparency? And beneath the clear bright surface, depths of purity which enabled her to flow through all experience, unchanged and always restful? If so, no wonder she attracted men.

But she was waiting.

"Mrs. Mallory, psychiatrists don't try to make people over," he said at last. "What they are, they are. And"—he hesitated, hating to disturb that soft credulity—"his recovery, this change in him has been abrupt. Indeed, the other night I had to readjust, as I have said, certain preconceived ideas I had had about him. Do I make myself clear?" he asked.

"No. Not entirely." She smiled.

"I had thought him vague and humbler than he acted. But the other night he acted neither vague nor humbled. Now, Mrs. Mallory, don't be alarmed. Certain personality changes often do occur, under shock, for instance, or when the consciousness of reality first returns. Your husband has been *very* ill." He paused. "Frankly, what concerns me is this. The fact that he snapped back so suddenly, and the fact that he is different, well, may I call it in emotional tone, leads me to wonder if the cure is permanent. Whether he is not just pretending now, talking like a parrot." She looked up. "I've said this to the General. I'd hoped he would relay it."

"He didn't," she said. "He didn't." She sighed. "But I understand. And I trust *you*."

"Time alone will tell."

"Of course, of course. Then it might be weeks and weeks yet?"

"Time will tell," he said again. She walked in silence, and the darkness shielded her face. "Meanwhile the General has a squad of men, I'm sure, out after Mr. Arbuthnot." He smiled. "And you don't have to wear a red camellia."

Coming under a street lamp, he could see the dimples. Light filled her eyes again.

"Wasn't I foolish? I'm sorry." Then—impulsively, "What a *nice* person you are, Doctor."

The next dark blocks were devoted to a very earnest catalogue of the sick man's likes and dislikes. As though she were not only embarrassed by her quick compliment, but making up for any spoken or implied criticism of her husband's personality, she began to pour out details to show that Eric Mallory had had interests outside his work, and had been "human."

It might help the doctor with his treatments, she explained. Her husband did read non-scientific books occasionally. History and books on economics mostly. He didn't care for fiction. He was very fond of chewing gum, but he didn't smoke or drink, and he sometimes looked at television, the program Omnibus. The doctor heard about Eric Mallory's allergy to wool, his hearty dislike for chicken or Italian food, his rather piteous attempt one spring to become interested in gardening, his awkward attempts to play ball with his son, and his strong but non-militant admiration of Adlai Stevenson.

They arrived at last before the house.

Lights were in the windows up and down the street. Lights were burning in the parlor beyond the porch.

"Would you like to stay for supper, Doctor?"

"You're very kind," he said. "I'm afraid I can't. I have an appointment," he went on, although he had none.

"We're having nothing very exciting tonight, but I would love to have you."

"Thanks very much, Mrs. Mallory, but I guess not."

He walked up to the door with her. In the room beyond the porch, he could see through the uncurtained windows the boy and the back of a large dark man in shirt sleeves, seated before the television set.

"I'm sorry," she said. "Dr. Fenton, this has meant a lot to me."

She stood a step higher than he—her head still below his own. Her face uptilted framed by the violet scarf, her eyes on which the light of the street lamp fell reminded him once more of a religious painting—the Madonna, or an angel. Angela. The name was most appropriate. Angela Romagna—an Italian girl, but one of ancient dynasty, rare blood. A Renaissance Italian, Florentine, Venetian. Faces like this had peered from palace windows, swept by in gilded barges, posed for Raphael and Michelangelo. He heard a gale of laughter from the television.

"When will you be leaving?"

"Oh, maybe in a week, ten days. As soon as my brother goes."

"You'll be hearing from the General, I feel sure. And I hope the news continues to be good."

She offered her hand.

"Good night, Mrs. Mallory."

"Good night, sir."

EIGHTEEN

He went home and fixed supper for himself, eating it alone in a silent house. Louisa was at the movies, and the parrot was morose. The doctor was stirring his second cup of coffee, lost in thought, when the telephone rang. It was the General.

"Are you alone, Fenton?"

"Yes. Are you in New York, sir?"

"No. I'm calling from Washington." His voice faded. "This is a hell of a connection. Is this better?"

"Fine now."

"I've been down below there, spending the day with him. With *him*," the General repeated, "and I thought it was important to have a word with you. He's an utterly changed human being, Fenton. To my mind he is cured. He's humble, eager to make amends, very grateful, full of firewater and vinegar, ready to go back to work. So I think it's important that we start thinking in terms of a clearance date."

When the doctor hesitated, the General continued, and tonight there was nothing ministerial in his tone. His voice was clipped and brisk.

"I know this seems hasty to you. But bad weather is coming. It snowed down there this morning. We'll have to move him and the whole shebang in any case . . . *somewhere*. And I say why not close up shop?"

"I'm afraid it's too early, General. My feeling is that he should be detained a little . . ."

"Hell, man," the General broke in, his voice crackling. "We can't speak of detaining a sane man. He's no prisoner of war, after all. He has certain rights. We don't want any stink raised." His voice faded, and when it came in clearly again, he was in the middle of a sentence. ". . . political considerations involved. Fenton? God *damn* this connection."

"I can hear you," the doctor said. "Are you proposing then that I don't see him any more . . . that we wash it up here and now?"

"Do you know of any good reason why we shouldn't?"

There was a belligerence in the last question that he resented. Co-operation seemed to be disintegrating. The General was showing his brass. But after all, it was no minister who had throttled those Nazis bare-handed.

The doctor kept his voice steady. "Yes, sir," he said. "I can think of several good reasons. It was my understanding when I left the other night that there would be two more interviews at the least. I think it's very important that we go through with them."

At the other end of the line he heard a heavy, distinctly exasperated sigh.

"Fire or no fire," he went on, "the transition seems much too abrupt. I feel it should be thoroughly tested. I fully realize that I'm not the final authority in this matter, either. All I'm doing is giving you my medical opinion."

"I can appreciate that, Fenton." The General's tone was finally conciliatory. "I don't mean to imply any lack of appreciation for your work. It's just that . . ." He paused. He was silent for so long that the doctor thought the connection had been broken. Finally the General said, "That place has to be closed down by Friday at the very latest. If weather permits, we'll have two more sessions. Otherwise only one. That's the best I can offer."

"Suppose the weather is so bad that we can't get through at all," the doctor said.

"We'll cross that bridge when we come to it," the General said. "Make it La Guardia, the old spot, at seven sharp tomorrow night."

Next morning it began to snow.

It was still snowing at seven that evening. He showed up

at La Guardia anyway. He and Stevens trudged across the field through swirling flakes to the plane. Nothing was coming in or going out, Stevens said, but the plane was being warmed up, apparently ready to go. The pilot was standing outside, and the doctor met him for the first time.

He was a young Negro in an Air Force uniform. Stevens drew him aside to talk it over. The doctor caught "clearance at our own risk" and "worse down there," and he thought he heard "land in the creek." Then Stevens returned, shrugging and shaking his head.

"He says we shouldn't risk it. Zero ceiling all the way down. Sorry, Doctor."

Tuesday the blizzard ended, but it became bitterly cold. Ice formed a jeweled crust over the snow, and the wind howled relentlessly. But Stevens telephoned at three, and said, "Are you game to try it this evening, Doctor? The General got through, and the pilot's willing to try."

In that milder climate of the blindfold country, the wind was more merciful. Snow *had* fallen here, but it was powdery, not frozen. It crept above his trouser cuffs and soaked his feet. But the concrete road seemed to have been cleared, and the station wagon sped over it as fast as usual. Only in the wooded area did he feel the presence of the snow again. Heavy clumps of it seemed to be falling from the trees as they passed through. And snow again slipped into his shoes as they left the bridge and went through the boxwood garden. Even before Stevens removed the blindfold, the General was brushing snow from the doctor's topcoat, helping him off with it, eager to begin.

Making it clear that he no longer intended to be a mere observer, the General planted himself in a chair, close to the screen, and signaled Major Brown to roll back the doors.

The mechanism was in working order again. Over the amplifier the voice sounded mechanical and precise, and it was chilly with distaste.

"I am well," he announced at once, paying no return to Dr. Fenton's salutation. "I want to be let out of here. I don't want psychoanalysis."

He then embarked on a didactic self-analysis, replete with terminology.

"I had an unfortunate neurological disturbance," he said haughtily. "Which a sensitive man, with a high-powered set of nerves and much responsibility, should be entitled to. But it has passed. And I don't intend to discuss the things I said during this period of amnesia. They are garbage, utterly non-germane to my conscious personality. My conscious is in fine working order again. If I wish to explore my subconscious in the next few years, I will consult an analyst of my own choosing."

When he was reminded of "murder" and of "Wichita Falls," he turned more huffy.

"But," the General broke in with apparent concern, "you realize that you did seem upset about those matters. You even suggested that we take your family to the moon."

"I think," the patient said significantly, "that you, General, will be able to understand what that particular reference might derive from. And as for Wichita Falls . . ."

"Yes," said the doctor, "what about Wichita Falls?"

"A little jerkwater town in Texas, where my wife and I spent a very brief time."

"Do you recall a Mr. Arbuthnot?" the doctor asked.

The General cleared his throat, scowling as if accusing the doctor of having improperly invaded the realm of security.

"Sure, I remember him," the patient said. "A two-bit physicist from Australia who's a bug on sports cars. I was thinking of buying a Jaguar at the time, and he took me for a ride in his. My wife didn't like him."

"Why didn't she?" the doctor asked.

"I think he made a pass at her and she resented it. How is she? Does she miss me?"

To Fenton, his voice had become disgustingly full of a sly innuendo.

"Mrs. Mallory is well," said the General, "and misses you very much."

"I should think so after all this time . . . Listen, General," he whined, and he seemed to be moving toward the screen; the canvas sneakers squeaked. "Is it fair, aside from my importance to the country, to keep me from my wife? I haven't heard from her in forever. I don't know what she's doing. You know the kind of attention she attracts, and she's very helpless in that type of situation." His voice caught in his throat. "Anything might be happening. *She* hasn't any judgment."

"Now . . . now . . ." the General said. He jerked his chair closer to the screen.

"Believe me"—the voice almost broke into a sob—"my family needs me. I keep worrying about my boy. I miss that little shaver. He needs a great deal of special attention too, you know that, General. Treatments. Sitting up at night. And my poor wife needs her rest."

The doctor listened, disbelieving.

"Take your damned psychiatrist and shove him," cried the patient. "I don't need all this nonsense. Let me go back to them, and live a normal life—and you can depend on me to deliver for my country."

Unable to conceal the cynicism in his voice, the doctor said, "All that you say may be perfectly legitimate, but it does not alter the fact that you still choose to wear a pillowslip over your head."

"What?" bellowed the patient. "You mean they haven't told you?"

"The pillowslip is off," said the General. "Dr. Throckmorton replaced it with a bandage."

"Then his face is still masked?" the doctor asked.

"Not a mask, it's a bandage," the patient said hostilely.

"Why?" Ignoring him, the doctor confronted the General. "Do you intend to release a masked man to his wife and job?"

"No," came the voice from behind the screen. "Of course not. I shall remove it as soon as my present skin condition has cleared up."

"What's this about a skin condition?"

"When the pillowslip was removed," the General replied, "Dr. Throckmorton found that the patient, in spite of all our efforts to keep him clean during his—er—period of forgetfulness, has unfortunately broken out with contact dermatitis.

Dr. Throckmorton had quietly entered the room.

"Am I right, Bill?"

"Yes, sir." The old man appeared very embarrassed. His face was beet-colored above the long white coat. "I took the mask off yesterday, and the poor man's face was just appalling. Blotches and lesions, some of them suppurating, especially about the eyes and nose."

Dr. Throckmorton was almost senile in his manner. Base X seemed to have added twenty years to his original sixty-six.

"That pillowslip got so dirty. And I foolishly used wool blankets. He has an allergy to wool . . ."

The doors were closed. The General turned to Dr. Fenton. "Well . . . ?"

Stevens appeared with the doctor's hat, coat and blindfold.

"We'll be with you in a second, Stevens," the General said, dismissing him. "Well, Doctor?"

"Of course under ordinary circumstances . . ." the doctor began.

The General banged his hand with his fist. "That's just it, Doctor. These are *not* ordinary circumstances. What you seem to forget is that you were *not* retained to do a complete analysis on this man."

"I haven't lost sight of that, sir."

"You were asked to put a genius back on the job." The General started pacing, smoothing his hair with both hands. "The man is perfectly sane. He has assured us of his loyalty over and over again. He is ready to return to work. Great issues are at stake. I don't expect you to comprehend them fully, but, please, for God's sake, take my word for it. Let's put him back in business."

When the doctor hesitated, the General went on with exasperation. "Let *me* handle spy rings in my own way, Doctor. *I'll* catch them all in time." He walked to the mantel, turned. "Let's sweep the board clean. To delay is only giving them further chances." He tapped his foot, his hands behind his back. "Well . . . ?"

"I'll be prepared to give you a complete summary of my feelings and conclusions after the next session," the doctor said stubbornly. "Meaning the final session, I suppose."

"Stevens," the General called, "the doctor's coat."

"Will it be tomorrow night?" the doctor asked.

"We'll let you know," the General said.

NINETEEN

When the doctor arose next morning, he learned that during the night the temperature had dropped to ten degrees. It had been an extraordinary November.

Yet it did not snow again during the day. The weather seemed no more unsuitable for flight than that of the previous evening. All through the day he waited for Stevens to call.

There was no call from Stevens, but at nine that evening, as he sat brooding in the library, there was one from Angela Mallory.

"Dr. Fenton, I'm leaving for home tomorrow, and I didn't want to go without telling you good-bye and thanking you."

"Tomorrow?" he asked sharply.

"Yes." She laughed lightly. "I had a call from the General this morning, asking me to take the first train I could get. You see I really ought to get the house ready. I'm sure the dust must be three inches deep down there. I have an awful lot to do before Saturday."

"Saturday?"

"The General said he hoped they could bring him home on Saturday. Anyway, by Sunday at the latest."

"Well . . ." he said, and paused. Hot blood had risen to his face, and his fingers gripped the receiver. He felt not only anger but a personal loss, and beyond these feelings, a sense of dark foreboding. But if the General had said to come, it was certainly not his place to say no, stay. Or to communicate even a hint of his own uneasiness. Eric Mallory was her husband, and who was he to tell her that her husband was a bastard.

"Well—have a good trip," he said at last.

"Good-bye, Doctor."

"Good-bye, good luck," he said.

"Thank you." She hung up.

He was the hired help, that was about the size of it.

But in the ensuing hours, he could not bear his silent house. He turned the hi-fi on, full blast, to Beethoven, then turned it off. He prowled the rooms, began a mystery novel, tossed it on the floor. Plunging out at last into the dark cold streets, he tried, with walking, both to dismiss her from his thoughts and to assess his thoughts about her. He thought of calling Monica, dropping in at Monica's very chic and gay apartment, but that was unfair to Monica. He went into a Third Avenue bar, staying there till closing time.

All the next day, Thursday, he kept thinking of her on the train, riding off to shadowland. He saw her turning a key, her little boy beside her . . . Angela in an apron, pitching in to clean up dust that "must be three inches deep . . ."

Thursday was notable for other reasons as well.

Leaving his office at seven after a purposely strenuous day, he had the sensation that he was being shadowed. The lobby was dim. The downstairs floor contained a drugstore, now closed, and there were alcoves and corridors leading to other offices. The man, his face half concealed by a hat pulled low, appeared to have been watching for him from the drugstore entrance. As Dr. Fenton swung on past it toward the street and the cab stand, he heard footsteps following. He turned. The man was looking into a display window. But when the doctor moved, the steps began again.

He did not stop, and a cab was waiting. He got in. But after supper, going to his parlor window to check the weather, he saw the man again. It was the same figure, he was sure, a man of average height, bundled in a heavy coat, pacing the sidewalk on this bitter night. The doctor drew the shades and turned away. This was absurd. His nerves were cracking. Anybody shadowing him certainly wouldn't be so obvious about it. When he looked again, the man was gone.

About ten o'clock the telephone rang.

"Hello."

No answer. The line was open. He could hear heavy breathing, irregular and harsh.

"Hello. What do you want?"

Just the breathing, and then a click.

A coincidence? Some drunken fool?

Ten minutes later, while he was reading in the library, the phone rang once again.

There was still the hope it might be Stevens.

"Hello."

Again the heavy breathing and a sort of grunt.

"Who is this?"

128

He waited only a second or two more, then disgustedly slammed down the phone.

When Stevens called again, he would tell him all about these spooks. Much more of this damned stuff, he thought, and they'll have *me* behind a screen.

If Stevens called, he amended. He was beginning to doubt that he would. He felt certain now that the General had by-passed him, taking matters into his own hands, that he wasn't even going to be allowed the final session the General had promised.

And if so, the hell with it; the hell with the General and with everybody else. Except Angela Mallory.

Friday morning another blizzard hit the city. While he was eating breakfast, Edna Willoughby called from Astoria. Her throat was sore. She thought she had best stay home, particularly since she had no dog sled.

He managed to get to the office by ten-thirty. He had a patient scheduled for eleven, but she didn't show up.

Just before eleven there was a phone call, just like the two he had had the previous evening. The caller was a man; that much he could determine from the deep, chesty breathing.

After lunch there was another call. This time the breathing had a quality of panting. The caller still did not speak.

His only patient of the day was with him from two till three. After she left, he stood at the window, watching the snow. It was not so heavy now. There were few cars moving. The streets were almost deserted. Although it was still early, there were lights already on in the apartment building across the way. As he watched, he saw something catch the light. He looked more closely. At a window stood a man with a pair of binoculars, trained, or so it seemed, directly on him.

He closed the blinds and slumped at his desk.

And presently, in the silence of the office, he laughed aloud. He remembered what the General had said about two weeks in Jamaica. At the moment it seemed like the best idea in months.

He looked again from the window. The man with the binoculars was gone. Not yet four o'clock, and already the street lights were on. He decided to close up shop and go home. It was a feat even to have opened. Most offices in the building were closed, or so the elevator operator had told him at lunchtime.

As he was putting on his coat, he heard the distant crash of the elevator, and then footsteps hesitantly approaching. They stopped, then came on again.

Cursing his own edginess, he listened intently. It could be a patient, couldn't it? Or . . .

It was a long time since he had even thought of a man named Green.

The footsteps paused outside his door. Then the doorknob turned and a man entered.

"Greetings." He was a tall and handsome man, flashily dressed in black, with a smile of great bravado. "You Dr. Fenton?"

"Yes."

"Pleased to meet you—finally." He extended a gray-gloved hand, blocking the door which he had contrived to close behind him. His dark eyes, melodramatic, sensual, roved past the doctor's head. He fumbled in his pocket, and striking a dramatic pose, flourished a small card. "The name is Romagna, Doctor."

It was there in print. Victor Romagna. "Lighting Fixtures" was printed underneath the name, and the Brooklyn telephone number. The card looked old.

"I'm Angie's brother, Doctor. Or Mrs. Mallory, if you prefer." The emphasis on her married name was flat. "Sorry I didn't get the opportunity—previously." He sat down. Still not bothering to remove his hat, he began to peel off his gloves. On his fingers were several rings.

Last Sunday, separated by the portieres, Dr. Fenton had

had an impression of a brother, oafish and guttural. Angela had seemed to keep him out of sight purposely. But this guy had a breezy suaveness. He reminded the doctor of men who operated around Rockefeller Center, furtively offering bargain diamonds.

"I got a proposition to make to you, Doc. Is anybody around?"

"Did Mrs. Mallory send you?"

"Angie? No—for God's sake!" Again he flashed the smile, knowing, cocksure, and perhaps attractively boyish in its day. But its day had gone. "Angie's left town. It's strictly my own idea, Dr. Fenton, or rather a whole *lot* of people's idea." He swept off the hat, revealing hair that had not grayed, hair that was as black and luxuriantly thick as hers. "Everybody loves my sister Angie."

He smiled again.

"I think you like her yourself." His smile was bordering on a leer. "You want to see the girl's protected."

"What's the point, Mr. Romagna?"

"Well, it's quite a point, Dr. Fenton . . ." Breathing deeply, expanding his broad chest, he rose. His nostrils flared. He tapped one finger on a coat button. "I realize I gotta appeal to your *heart* rather than to your head. You know? Although I got proof along those lines, if you are interested. But it's an *honest* offer."

"What are you talking about?"

"Angie, she's my sister, see?" He advanced. "But she don't ask me anything. She's a Romagna, too. But does she ask the family anything? No." He shrugged contemptuously. "She listens to the government. And what's the government gonna do for Angie? Sell her down the river, that's what the government's gonna do."

It was a violent little speech, but he looked sincere as he spoke it. The doctor began to soften his first estimate. Perhaps Mr. Romagna had looked too long at television.

"What do you mean, Mr. Romagna?"

"I mean"—the words were blurted out—"her husband's crazy. He oughta be *kept* locked up.

"*Now*," he continued before the doctor could protest, "you think I should have spoken up before. I should have called you up. The fact is, I thought of it. But the kid tells me you're a great guy, a great doctor. You'd do a complete job, leave you alone, she tells me. Everybody figured it's gonna take much longer. Then all of a sudden, bam, it happens. She tells me he's coming back to her on Saturday night." His eyes bulged at the doctor, accusing eyes. "My sister's getting back her crazy husband tomorrow night. That's twenty-four hours from now."

"Now, Mr. Romagna," said the doctor. "You have no proof of his condition . . ." But he spoke without conviction. The words just said were an echo of his thoughts.

"You don't cure a lunatic like *him* . . ." Romagna began. He broke off suddenly. He stared around the silent office. "Doctor, I don't know your business, and far be it from me to give you any technical argument. It's the heart I gotta appeal to. She's my *sister*—and I practically raised her." Hard to believe. Again he touched the coat button. "You maybe got a sister yourself. Could you stand by and see her ruining her life?"

"What makes you think she's ruining it?"

"I *know* she's ruining it," said his caller forcefully. He waved his hands. "Listen, I followed that marriage for seven years. And God, even when he's *sane*, he's nutty. Listen, Doc, I'm no psychiatrist, but I know women. I've seen what he did to Angie, wore her down, left her alone. Half the time he didn't even sleep with her. And jealous. What's he got a right to be jealous of? You ask me, he's a eunuch."

"A eunuch." The doctor smiled faintly. That did not sound like the *recent* patient, certainly. And, coming from Victor Romagna, there was the question of degree.

"Sure. What does he live for? His laboratory. What does he talk about? The stars. He's got a crazy look in his eye. Just to have married her shows he was crazy. Picking out a doll like Angie, a sweet, religious girl, she could have married a millionaire. You know where he plans to take her, don't you? The moon." He spoke with scorn. "She's gonna be the first woman who can get there. That's nice. And he *believes* it."

His visitor shrugged bitterly. "So—maybe it's a possibility. Who cares? Who needs it?" His dark eyes shifted.

"The world has changed, Mr. Romagna . . ."

"Yeah, to hell with it." His visitor studied him, then grinned. "I think you agree," he stated with another smile.

"Agree with what?"

"That you don't release him?"

"Mr. Romagna . . ."

"Okay, okay." The smile stayed fixed. "You don't have to tell me yes or no. I'm not the General or the government. Just —wiggle out of it. You know. He needs more treatment. And I won't remember I was ever here."

He picked up his hat.

"Mr. Romagna, I have not said—"

"Sure—sure." He put his hat on. "Nothing unethical," he soothed. "Strictly on the up-and-up. You think about it." He fumbled in his coat pocket. "Well, I've taken up a lot of your time, Doctor. You're a busy man."

Blandly, he looked around the office, then, with a deft turn, laid something down on Edna's desk blotter. He backed with swiftness toward the door and opened it.

"Hey, wait a minute," cried the doctor.

Mr. Romagna waved a hand. "Consultation fee." He winked. "Thanks." He vanished.

"Listen—"

The doctor ran out of the office after him. But he had evidently ducked down the service stairs. The corridor was empty.

He walked slowly back to his office, and with the door closed counted the bills.

They were in tens and fives, well worn, and totaled five

hundred and fifty dollars. They had been tied together with a piece of string. He put them finally into his safe.

TWENTY

When he left the office, it was dark and the snow had stopped. The air was softer, and a few stars were out. Unable to find a taxi, he walked morosely home through a city strangely silent, muffled by the snow.

At 86th Street he bought a newspaper. The headline said: "Freak Storm Blitzes East."

Louisa had the television set on. He heard a commentator intoning: "Trucks jackknifed . . . hundreds of cars stalled . . . wires down in the suburbs . . ."

Louisa said there had been no calls all day.

While waiting for supper he called Edna to see how she felt, then had her call him back to make sure his telephone was working.

It was after eleven and he had been in bed an hour when the telephone awakened him. His first thought was of Stevens.

"Hello . . ."

For answer, only heavy breathing.

"*Hell*—lo," he said and waited. The sounds went on, and then stopped. The clock in his bedroom ticked like a time bomb.

In a vague way he had blamed Victor Romagna for the previous calls. But not now.

"Speak up!" he shouted. "This is Richard Fenton. What do you want?"

A long silence, and then choked sounds. It was as though

an overgrown Mongoloid were sobbing, gasping at the other end.

The sounds were familiar . . . somehow.

He felt a sudden chill. A trickle of sweat ran down one arm.

"Mallory!" he shouted.

The gagging became more intense.

"Is this Eric Mallory?"

He waited, sweated as he listened.

"Mallory," he said gently. "This is Doctor Fenton. Please tell me where you are."

"Deposit ten cents for the next three minutes, please," a female voice broke in.

"Operator," the doctor said, "stay off the line, please. Mallory . . ."

But there was another gasp, a kind of clatter. The caller had hung up.

Slowly he placed the receiver back in its cradle, then immediately picked it up again, dialing the operator.

"I just had a call," he said, giving his number. "Is it possible for it to be traced?"

"I'm sorry, sir, but that's impossible."

"Suppose it had been long distance? Would there be a record?"

"You would have to know the city your party was calling from."

But of course it was not long distance. The operator flashed and asked for another dime that way only on local calls. Mallory must be in New York.

Hanging up at last, the doctor sat despondently on the edge of the bed.

Mingled with the shock and concern was a nasty vindictive little twinge of triumph. The General knew so damned much!

Cured, eh? Well the "cure" had been damned brief.

But why New York? And how had he gotten to New

York? Had he run away? And why had he called here? Why not the Romagna house?

And where in God's name was the General? Out playing pinochle?

Still he sat there, hopeful that the phone would ring again, juggling all the possibilities.

Mallory did not know that Angela had gone to her mother's. Nor had he ever liked the Romagnas. In addition to which the house was empty. The phone was disconnected now. So— knowing Fenton's name, and remembering that Fenton had been helpful, had been instrumental in helping him over-come his inability to speak at Base X, it was natural enough . . .

If, that is, it had been Mallory. The doctor lit a cigarette, and lay propped up in bed. After all, he had not even heard a voice. It could be another trick. Fitzgerald had been an artist at impersonation.

For a long while he lay there, frowning at the ceiling, deep in concentration. Presently he dozed off.

Toward four he came awake again as if he had been pro-pelled, and it seemed that the truth of the matter took form, was laid clear and plain before him just in the few seconds it took to pass from sleep to wakefulness.

It would explain the sudden arrogance and nastiness—quali-ties which certainly had not been apparent in the original patient, and which did not fit Angela's description of her hus-band's nature. It would explain Dr. Fenton's own abrupt switch from sympathy for his patient to deep repugnance. It would even explain the pat familiarity with psychiatric terms.

The lamp beside his bed was still on. He reached for a ciga-rette, turned out the lamp and lay smoking in the dark.

Down the street he heard a snow plough and the rasp of shovels.

Dr. Fenton slept no more that night. For two hours he lay there, trying to figure out every facet. Toward seven he got up, shaved, took a shower and dressed.

Strong doubt by now had set in. Mallory, after all, had been under constant guard, attended by orderlies around the clock. Base X was an island, manned by sentries. It would have been next to impossible to make a switch.

He studied his own face. Near-doubles of course could be found. Somewhere in the world there was a face that might pass as a fair duplicate of the weary countenance looking back at him from the mirror.

But the variation in human faces was infinite, and to find an identical replica seemed unlikely. Plus, a voice and some familiarity with science. Of course, most of the time the *face* had been covered up, conveniently, by a pillowslip. But that pillowslip had been removed. Dr. Throckmorton himself had removed it, had seen the man, had treated the skin rash and bandaged the face again.

But if the explanation was that Mallory had had a relapse and escaped, then why in God's name hadn't the General called him? Maybe, he thought wryly, the answer was simply that he had been fired for insubordination.

Down in the kitchen he slid two pieces of bread into the toaster, started the burner under last night's coffee and placed a person-to-person call to the General at the Pentagon.

The switchboard operator transferred the call to Pentagon information.

There was no extension listed.

He had expected none. He canceled the call.

While his mouth was full of toast, the telephone rang. The voice was deferential and precise.

"Is this the residence of Dr. Richard Fenton? This is he? This is the Hotel Colton, Doctor. Sorry to disturb you at this hour, but I'm calling to see if you might be able to help us. Do you know a man named Mulroy?"

The doctor gulped down the toast. "Could it be *Mallory?*" he asked excitedly.

"Conceivably," the man said. "Yes, conceivably it might be Mallory. He has written it on a slip of paper and his handwriting is quite shaky, quite illegible. He has been here since five o'clock this morning."

"Is he there now?"

"Yes, you see he apparently has a severe case of laryngitis or the like because he's unable to talk. He's—"

"Thank you," the doctor said "I'll be right there."

The Colton was in the Murray Hill section. It was of Gothic architecture with an elaborate porte-cochere. Within, the lobby was dim, oak-paneled. But not a sofa or a chair was occupied. Behind a counter carved like an altar, a balding, immaculately dressed young man was sorting mail. He looked up.

"I'm Dr. Fenton. Where is he?"

"Oh yes, Doctor. I'm terribly sorry." The young man spread his hands, assuming a look of amazement. "He ducked *out*. While I was talking to you on the telephone. I tried to reach you but your maid said you had left."

"Just in the ten minutes it took me to get here? He disappeared?"

"Yes. Incredible." The desk clerk snapped his fingers. "Just like that. One minute he was here, the next he wasn't."

The doctor slumped wearily against the counter. A tall mahogany clock nearby began to chime. It was seven-thirty.

"Poof!" the young man said, waving a pale hand. "Gone! And this after so *tenaciously* refusing to *budge* from that chair since five this morning."

"Could you tell me how he was dressed?"

"Umm," the clerk said. "I should say *incongruously*. That is, he was dressed like a longshoreman, or whatever those fellows are called, and yet he looked like anything *but* a longshoreman. One of those abbreviated blue jackets and a knit cap. His trousers were positively stiff as a *board*. He looked as if he might have fallen into the river."

"Thank you," the doctor said, and hurried out into the street. Glancing north and south on Madison, he set out at a brisk pace, circling first the immediate block, then others, working outward at an ever-widening radius from the hotel. Finally he returned.

"Oh, *there* you are, Doctor." The clerk clipped his fountain pen on his shirt pocket. "Any trace?"

"No," the doctor said. "I wonder if you could tell me what he looked like. I mean aside from his clothing."

"Umm . . ." The clerk tilted his chin, supporting it with his thumb. "Umm . . . blond," he snapped decisively. "He didn't remove the cap, but I had a distinct impression of blondness. Blond stubble. He needed a shave. A rather slightly built man. The jacket was far too large for him . . . **Doctor**, if I had suspected he had the slightest intention of ducking out, I should most certainly have had someone sit on him, as it were."

"Not at all," the doctor said. "You've been very co-operative. Now . . . I wonder if by any chance you have the memo —the piece of paper he wrote my name on."

"Gee . . ." The young man swept a hand over the counter, turned, looked behind him, then swept the counter again. "Well . . ." he said, bending out of sight. From the sound, he seemed to be rummaging in a trash basket.

His head popped into view. "*Voilà!*" He handed the doctor a rumpled sheet of hotel stationery. The doctor smoothed it on the counter. A word that most certainly looked more like Mulroy than Mallory. Other scratching.

"May I have this?" he asked.

The clerk shrugged. "Why not?"

The doctor went into a Nedick's, ordered coffee and smoothed out the paper on the counter. The name, written three times, in a palsied hand. Then the words "Single room. I have stayed here before. Please."

The last word was underlined. The doctor had a momentary glimpse of Eric Mallory, in knit cap and pea jacket, looking up pleadingly at the clerk.

And when the clerk had said nothing was available, he must

have written the next words "Dr. Rich Fenton," with the correct phone number, followed by the words "Reference—vouch."

And at the very bottom the number 46 with an indecipherable word before it. Perhaps the number of the room that Mallory and Angela had shared in happier days.

The doctor sipped his coffee thoughtfully, studying the word. No, it was not "room." Nor was it "number." The first letter was a p.

Could it be "pier"?

Pier 46?

That was certainly what it appeared to be. But why? And why all this business about longshoremen and longshoremen's paraphernalia?

The doctor drained the cup and caught a taxi. "Pier 46, North River," he said.

It was still not quite eight-thirty.

Untrodden snow lay before the huge gray shed. The gates were locked. No ships lay in the slips. On this clear bright winter morning, the Intercontinental Import-Export Company looked as though all its business might be out on the high seas.

Its ports of call had a Conradian flavor: Manila, Hong Kong, Bombay, Calcutta.

The doctor looked through a window, hoping to find a bulletin board or something that might list a sailing schedule.

He turned away. A cold wind was blowing from the river, whipping at his topcoat. A tug was passing just beyond the end of the slip. Its whistle blasted hoarsely, and a sea gull took flight from a piling and flapped after the tug.

The tug was headed upstream and three blocks or so to the north he could see bustling activity at another pier. A continuous flow of taxis, stopping to discharge passengers and luggage. Smoke, bent by the wind from two orange stacks, drifted toward the city. A liner leaving for the Caribbean perhaps, for a winter cruise.

The Caribbean, where, if he had followed the General's suggestion, he might now be.

He turned from the shed. Maybe he could get a listing from the *Times* shipping desk. Intent now on finding a taxi, he saw a man stoop and pick a cigarette butt from the gutter.

The doctor approached. The man was squinting at the butt, seemingly disgusted at its length. He wore a knit cap and a faded tan jacket over a turtle-neck sweater. "Can you tell me anything about this line here?" the doctor asked, offering him a cigarette. The man took two, and looked up, on the defensive. "Anything in or out recently?"

"Had one go out last Monday and another one go out yesterday morning. No. Morning before last."

"Do you know the name of that one?"

"On Thursday morning? She was . . ." The man frowned and rubbed at the white stubble that covered his chin. "*Star of* . . . *Star of* some damned thing. I forget."

"Do you know where she was headed?"

"Far East is all I know. All of 'em from that line go to the Far East."

"Thanks." The doctor offered the pack again. The man took three more. "Good luck," the doctor said and hailed a taxi.

"Good morning, Sergeant. My name is Fenton. M.D." The doctor opened his wallet and tugged out his A.M.A. membership card.

The sergeant looked at it without interest. He was a frail man who looked as if he might have an ulcer. Three half-pint cartons of milk were lined up before him on the desk, each with a straw.

"I just wondered," the doctor said, "if I could take a look at the ticker."

The sergeant waved his consent.

The teletype machine was pounding out a report on "Lawrence Hogan, W. M., 49 yrs." who had "jumped or fallen" from the roof of a building on Hudson Street. He was dead on arrival at St. Vincent's Hospital.

The doctor picked up the sheaf of reports from the previous days, and, beginning with 11:00 P.M. on Wednesday, he began leafing through the yellow sheets.

Presently he stopped. The report he was looking for was timed off at eleven o'clock Thursday morning. But the accident, if that was the proper word, had happened about three hours earlier.

An unidentified white male, approximately forty-five years old, weighing about 160 pounds and about five feet ten inches tall, had jumped or fallen from the deck of an outbound freighter, the *Star of Bombay*, just off the Battery. He had been picked up by a bargeman named Johannssen.

The doctor stood reading the report a second and then a third time. Then he asked the sergeant for permission to use a telephone directory. In the yellow section, he turned to the "J's."

Steam was coming from the stubby stack, and the coal barge seemed about ready to vacate the berth it occupied on the lower end of the East River.

"Are you Mr. Johannssen?" the doctor shouted.

A huge man in a blue-plaid shirt nodded, looked up from the stern line he had been about to cast off.

"Can I see you a minute?" the doctor called.

Mr. Johannssen seemed unenthusiastic. Dubiously he looked ahead toward the two scows, laden with coal and attached end to end, which he was set to shove from the berth. The lead scow's nose was sticking out into the river.

"Very important," the doctor shouted.

The giant mounted a pile of coal and peered again out toward the end of the slip. Then he clumped back to the deck, throttled down the engine, took a turn in the stern line and motioned the doctor to come aboard.

The doctor leaped the two feet separating the barge from the dock, stumbled a step or two and came up hard against the small cabin at the after end, feeling far from nautical.

"Sorry to hold you up like this," the doctor said. He introduced himself. Johannssen offered a huge hand. Pale blue eyes peered out from a face seamed with coal dust.

"I'd like to ask you something about that man you picked out of the river the other morning," the doctor said.

"Yeah, I picked him up down near the Battery. Are you his doctor?"

"That's right."

"He said he didn't want any doctor." Johannssen began to fill a corncob pipe. "I tried to get him a doctor."

"Can you tell me how it all happened?" Dr. Fenton asked.

"Well, it was about eight o'clock in the morning . . ."

About eight o'clock in the morning. Johannssen was just off the lower tip of Manhattan when he saw the man go over the side of the freighter, almost in the path of the Staten Island ferry. The ferry pilot had to back water and swerve. The freighter kept going.

"I signaled to the ferry that I'd pick him up. I threw him a line. By the time I get him aboard, the freighter's almost out to the Narrows, going like hell. It looked like they don't even notice he goes overboard."

Johannssen sat on a keg and lit the pipe.

"Did you catch the freighter's name?"

"*Star of Bombay*, she was." Johannssen shook his head. "Twelve degrees that morning. Enough to kill a man. Lucky I got to him as soon as I did. I guess he wasn't in the water more than five minutes at most. Good thing, too."

Johannssen had put in near the Fulton Fish Market and had gone ashore to call a doctor.

"I tell him to stay in the cabin and try to get warm. His lips were blue and his teeth were chattering and his eyes watering. Wonder he wasn't dead."

"So you went ashore?"

"Yeah, and when I get back he's gone. Disappeared. So I decide I better report it to the police." A moment longer Johannssen puffed reflectively at his pipe. "Poor little bastard," he said. "He was so cold he could hardly talk." Rising, he started to unhitch the stern line. "That's all I know about it," he said.

"You mean he *did* talk?" the doctor asked.

"He said something about going over to Red China to make spaceships for the Chinks. Said he was going to the moon. Hah! He had a very bad stuttering."

"Did he say anything else?"

"No. He just sits there with his teeth chattering." Johannssen dropped the line on the deck and stood holding the barge in with his huge hand over the piling.

"You'll have to excuse me now, Doctor. I'm late."

TWENTY-ONE

As the elevator clanged shut behind him, he heard the telephone ringing. He hurried for the door of the office, pulling his key case from his pocket.

But it was not Mallory.

"Dr. Fenton? Sergeant Oliver, East 51st Street. Say, Doc, do you know a man named Mulroy?"

"Could it be Mallory, Sergeant?" He began to perceive that the slight difference in names was not a garbling but Mallory's pitiable attempt at an alias.

"Might be. We've got it as Mulroy. We picked him up near the U.N. building early this morning, stretched out cold.

144

After we got him up here he said he was a patient of yours."

The other telephone began ringing.

"Right, Sergeant," the doctor said. "He's my patient. Thanks. I'll be right down."

"Wait! Hold it!" the sergeant said. "He's not here. We sent him down to Bellevue."

"Is he sick?"

"Sick and off his rocker both."

The other call was Louisa asking if the sergeant had reached him. The sergeant had tried him at home first.

"Why didn't you call me to get your breakfast?" Louisa said, and then began on the inadequacy of toast and coffee.

He cut her short.

Although he had never been on the staff at Bellevue, the doctor knew a psychiatrist there. He dialed the number swiftly.

"Dr. Adams, please."

A voice said, "Psychiatric."

"Dr. Adams, please. Dr. Richard Fenton calling."

"Dr. Adams will be in later. Could Dr. Willis help you?"

"Thanks, I'll speak to him."

"Dr. Willis speaking." It was a woman.

"Dr. Willis, this is Dr. Richard Fenton."

"Oh *yes*, Fenton." She was impressed.

"Do you have a patient there named Mallory? He might be listed as Mulroy. Sent over from the 51st Street station?"

"The one found near the U.N.? Yes, he's here. Is he your private patient, Doctor?"

"He is—a friend," he answered after a moment's pause. "How is he?"

"I haven't examined him personally, Doctor, but I understand his condition is critical. Severe exposure, I believe, and shock. I'll check."

She left the line and he waited. When she returned her voice was sympathetic.

"I'm awfully sorry, Doctor. It's pneumonia."

"I'll be right over, Dr. Willis."

He did not wait for the elevator. He took the service stairs, two at a time.

Dr. Willis was soft-spoken, intelligent and extremely feminine. Leading him down the corridor, she said, "I checked him over after I talked with you, Doctor. It's in both lungs."

"Dr. Adams will be in at eleven?"

"Maybe sooner. He's a hard worker."

He followed her into the ward.

It was jammed with beds, but clean and sunny. At this hour of the morning, most of the patients were wide awake—men of all ages, colors, sprawled on the beds, wandering about, reading newspapers or listening to their radios. Some called to Dr. Willis, but with her quick light step, she led the doctor on to a far corner.

Here under a high-barred window lay a man—with a blond-bearded face. He lay on his back. His eyes were closed. He was breathing laboriously through his mouth. A tiny pulse moved in his temple.

He had light brown hair, sparse across the top, and one stray lock of it lay across his brow. His features were finely chiseled.

"God . . ." Dr. Fenton breathed.

"Respirations are forty per minute and temperature is a hundred and four," said Dr. Willis, handing him the chart.

"A hundred and *four?*" Dr. Fenton said.

"Yes, I'm afraid so, Doctor. I think I'd better order the oxygen and antibiotics without waiting for Dr. Adams."

"Yes, please do."

She walked briskly away.

The breathing was very shallow. The hand upon the blanket looked very limp—a hand which quite obviously had never known much manual labor.

Dr. Fenton bent over the bed. "Good evening," he said. "I am Dr. Richard Fenton . . . I have come to help you."

He repeated the words—as close to his old manner as was possible—in a low voice. Once. Then twice.

The man inhaled. There was a flutter of the hand upon the sheet. Then the eyes opened. They were ice-blue, but deeply clouded now.

"F-Fenton . . . ?"

"Yes."

The eyes flickered over the doctor's face, in surprise, then disbelief, then trust. A feeble smile turned up the corners of the mouth. "T-thank you . . ." The eyes closed. The shallow breathing once again resumed.

The hesitancy, the humility, the feeling of essential decency. This was unmistakably the man that he had treated. The man he had *liked*. And that voice was *real*. Looking down at the heaving chest, he felt overwhelmed with pity.

An old man with bright eyes leaned up on one elbow in the adjoining bed. "Gone?" he chirped expectantly.

"No," said the doctor.

Dr. Willis was returning. Close behind her came the oxygen equipment. A mask was once more being placed over the face of Eric Mallory.

Outside in the corridor, Fenton drew Dr. Willis aside. "Doctor," he said, "I can't emphasize too strongly how vital it is to save this man. He is not only a close personal friend of mine. He is—" Dr. Fenton paused. Mallory, anonymous, was safer here than anywhere. "He is a man of extraordinary intellect. Great ability."

Behind the rimless glasses, her soft dark eyes grew softer.

"I'm not going to try to tell you how to run your business," Dr. Fenton said. "I'm not going to suggest specialists. I've got friends I might recommend, of course, but there's no better hospital than Bellevue, and I know you'll do all in your power. I might say that if a private room would help, please see that he gets one. Spare nothing. Whatever expense is involved, I'll pay personally."

"You know we'll do everything possible, Doctor."

"Thank you very much, Doctor. I'll keep checking."

TWENTY-TWO

Essential as Mallory's life might be, it was not the only life at stake. For if the doctor's calculations were correct, then Angela's life was at stake as well.

Dr. Fenton settled back in the cab, trying to relax, trying not to be irritated by the driver's crawling progress through the heavy crosstown traffic.

The morning was going. It had been early when that first call came. But more than three hours now had been consumed by that zigzag trail to—absolute proof. He had it now. There was no longer doubt in his mind. The evidence was overwhelming.

The arrogant, smug "Mallory," the man the General thought was "cured," had not been Mallory at all. And unless he was very much mistaken, he realized now how the switch had been accomplished.

The fire at Base X had been no accident. It had been started deliberately. With the fire as a cover, Dr. Eric Mallory had been smuggled out, taken to New York and held captive until the freighter was set to sail.

And in his place had been planted a man clever enough to deceive a whole staff of vigilantes. A man well grounded in the details even of Mallory's personal life. A man who must have been trained meticulously, and who had an untold advantage in that neither the General nor anyone else on the small hand-picked staff had ever known the real Mallory as a well man.

The pillowslip, the bandages, the skin rash, in fact the entire matter of Dr. Throckmorton's stewardship—these were still inexplicable points. He recalled Throckmorton's pronounced nervousness after the fire. It seemed inconceivable that a former army surgeon might have been an accomplice. But this was incidental now.

What mattered now was that on this very night, unknown to the General, a man of evil was going to be taken home to Angela Mallory, a man for whom she was preparing a homecoming in the belief that it was her husband. She would know he was a fake the moment she saw him. But by then the escort would have left, the doors would have closed upon the smiling General. And the fake, God knows, must have a plan. He must have faced long since this final test. Devised escape, with Angela as hostage, or a victim.

It was all veiled. It was unknown, in detail. But the double had just one night. He would be deep, deep in enemy territory, by now hell-bent for *any* out. Would one frail woman stop him? Not such a man, or such a group of men, who had risked so much and now deceived so many. The fact remained that unless Angela Mallory used her wits or possessed a gun, she would be dead by midnight at the very latest. She might be murdered simply to cover up the crime.

It was in his, Richard Fenton's, power, to save her life. All he had to do was get through to the General.

That's all.

"Good morning, Doctor." Fortified with a container of coffee, Edna was opening the mail.

"Good morning," he said absently, and swept past her desk into the consulting room. Closing the door, he dialed the operator and placed a call to Army Intelligence at the Pentagon.

He reached a Major Somebody.

"This is Dr. Richard Fenton in New York," the doctor said. "I'm trying to reach Lieutenant General Leonard Atwood. In fact, it's absolutely vital that I reach him, and I wonder if you could help me."

"I'm sorry, sir, but he has no office in this section."

"Do you know of a General Atwood?"

The major seemed to hesitate. "His name is not immediately familiar to me, sir."

"For *God's sake!*" the doctor exploded.

"Let me have you switched to Colonel Lawrence." The major flashed the operator. "Switch to 76432, please."

And then a woman's voice. "Colonel Lawrence's office."

"May I speak to Colonel Lawrence, please?"

"I'm sorry. Colonel Lawrence is not at his desk at the moment. May I help you?"

"I'm trying to reach a General Atwood. I was switched to Colonel Lawrence."

"General Atwell?" she asked.

"Atwood." Patiently he spelled it.

"Perhaps Colonel Lawrence can help you. Could you call back?"

"This *is* Army Intelligence, isn't it?"

"Yes, sir."

He sighed. "Could you take a message for Colonel Lawrence, please. This is Dr. Richard Fenton in New York. It is absolutely vital that I reach General Atwood. This is a matter of national emergency. Will you have Colonel Lawrence or somebody, anybody, do whatever can be done to have the General telephone me, please?"

"I'll be happy to give Colonel Lawrence your message."

He hung up and put his head in his hands, rubbing his eyes, massaging his temples.

Damn a system that involved a man deeply, that gave him crucial responsibility, and yet kept him blindfold, cut off as completely as if he had been on another planet.

A system that had outwitted itself by its very secrecy.

There was a tap at the door. Edna pushed it open. "Would you like some coffee, Doctor?"

"No, thanks," he said. "Yes, I think maybe I would. Wait a minute." Edna's presence was finally registering. "What are you doing in here on Saturday?"

She smiled. "We have some appointments today, Doctor. Don't you remember? The ones we canceled the day of the snow?"

"Oh, God," he groaned. "All right. We'll have to cancel them again."

"Are you sure, Doctor?"

"Yes. Cancel them for me, please . . . and then, if you could run down and get me some coffee . . ."

She closed the door and he reached behind him for the Brooklyn directory and checked the Romagna number again. The report, as before, was that the phone had been disconnected. Other Romagnas? They might be related. They might know the name of the town where Angela Mallory lived, even though it was a government installation. He tried four Romagnas. None had ever heard of Angela or Victor.

He sat drumming on the desk. So now what? Wait for the General to call willy-nilly? Or for the absent Colonel Lawrence to track him down? It was beginning to be doubtful, he thought grimly, that there *was* a General.

But of course there was a General. And wherever he might be, he'd certainly come running in response to a front-page headline, wouldn't he?

Maybe the surest way to flush the General out of limbo would be to call a newspaper or a wire service and spill the story.

He sat pondering the idea. But that would be assuming to himself authority and experience that he did not have. It was a story that could have untold consequences on an entire nation. It might even be construed as treason. There had been high policy, world policy behind that oath of secrecy. And he had taken that oath. The oath had not been lifted.

"A ruthless race . . ."

No. It was hope that Stevens or the General would call. Or that he could somehow reach Base X.

Base X.

That was where the General was, of course—incommunicado—supervising "Mallory's" departure. There. At Base X. Everybody was still at Base X. A place that possibly was a mystery to Intelligence proper, for it was no government installation, just an old rundown house. Base X was the point of stress, not Washington. If he could reach it before tonight, he could not only reach the General, he could stop the double . . .

He groaned silently.

By tonight. A house he had never seen. A place he had been taken to in a plane with sealed-up windows. Roads concealed from view by a blindfold. But—there were features of it that he knew. Things that he had learned through smell, through touch, through hearing. And there was one room he had *seen*.

A beautiful, an unusual room. Its details were as familiar as this office. Marvelous old wallpaper, a fine old chandelier, a marble mantel. It was a room that had known elegance. It existed now as in some fourth dimension. But *before* the General came, it must have had a history.

He sat a moment more. At first the scheme seemed too absurd, far-fetched. Not to mention time-consuming. But it was worth a try. Trying was better than sitting here all day.

"Edna." He walked excitedly to the outer office. "We need somebody to make telephone calls. Do you know somebody we could get here in a hurry?"

She frowned. "Here? For us? Just phoning? Well, my cousin Gloria . . ."

"Is she old enough to use the phone intelligently?"

"She's eighteen. Not terribly bright, but bright enough, I guess."

"How soon can you get her here?"

"If she's home and there's money involved, I'm sure she'd be able to get here in nothing flat." Edna smiled.

"There's money involved."

Returning to his consulting room, he telephoned Bellevue

and learned that Eric Mallory was still on critical, no better and no worse.

He then took a battered atlas from his shelves and spread it open on the desk.

". . . land in the creek." He recalled the pilot's words—the smell of swampy inland water, the footbridge and the gravel.

He traced the trickles and curves of blue. The state could be Virginia or Maryland or possibly even North Carolina. A two-hour plane ride in a two-engine plane—and south. The smell of honeysuckle, the warmer air—and that mosquito. He looked at the eastern arm of Maryland, a maze of rivers and creeks and coves and inlets. But on the other hand, the part of Maryland on the western side of the Chesapeake was very similar. And so was Virginia, both eastern shore and western shore.

On a sheet of his letterhead stationery he drew three columns, heading them Maryland, Virginia and North Carolina.

Twenty minutes later he was addressing Edna and the tall, dark young woman, who was her cousin Gloria.

"Can you type, Gloria?"

"No."

"All right then, Edna, you make a carbon, please." Edna slipped the paper into her machine. "Okay? Take this down."

"One: It is on an island off some woods in a cove or bay."

Edna looked up.

"Go on. Two: It is frame, old, and possibly eighteenth century.

"Three: It has a drawing room with Chinese wallpaper, red with a gold design of mandarins. There is a pier-glass mirror over the marble fireplace in this drawing room and a crystal chandelier."

"Should I number all these separate facts?" asked Edna. "Separate paragraphs?"

"It doesn't matter. Four—" he paused. "It is approached

by a short wooden footbridge, there is a lawn in front, a wooden picket gate, and then an old brick sidewalk leading to some shallow steps. It has a wide front porch.

"Five: One of the features is a boxwood garden in front. This boxwood is high and must be very old. It borders the brick sidewalk.

"Six: The house's furnishings include a pie-crust mahogany table, an antique, two blue wing chairs, possibly antiques, and an eighteenth-century pattern tea and coffee silver service."

"Doctor—" Edna Willoughby murmured.

"Keep on. Seven: It is about twenty minutes by car from a large estate or a country inn or summer resort." He stopped. Those voices that first night still seemed too fantastic. The General couldn't have picked a place that close to a public spot from which came so much sound. "No, take that out," he said. "That's all. Now, ladies . . ." He rolled the sheets from the machine. "One copy for each. Gloria, you can use this phone here. And now I'll explain." He smiled at them. "You ladies are going to buy a house today. *That* house. By noon, I hope."

"Are you getting *married*, Doctor?" Edna looked flabbergasted.

"No. This is a house I've seen. I like it, and I want it in a hurry."

"Where is it?" ventured Gloria, twisting her hair.

"That's a good question," the doctor said. "I don't know."

"You don't *know?*" Edna and Gloria exchanged glances.

He set the atlas before them. "I'm assuming it's in either Maryland, Virginia or North Carolina. It *has* to be. And it's up to you ladies to find it for me. Now I'm assuming again that the place I want is on the water, and I know it has to be within two-hundred fifty or three-hundred miles of New York. Now you'll see from this atlas that there are certain counties in both states that border the Chesapeake. I think this place is more likely to be on the Chesapeake side than on the ocean side. Are you following me?"

"Not exactly," said Edna. Gloria giggled.

"Okay," he said. "In any event I've picked out the counties I want, and I've made a list of them, and here's the list." He placed it on the desk. "I want you ladies to call up real-estate offices in each county and find that house."

"By *noon?*" Edna looked pained. "That's like trying to find a needle in a haystack."

"You are perfectly right," he told her, grinning. "But I want that house. And real-estate salesmen are amazing. They'll do anything to make a sale, and they have a knowledge of local lore and historical houses that beats any history book."

Edna finally managed her double take.

"But, Doctor, you said you'd *been* there."

"Yes," he said. "I have. And yet again I haven't."

Edna shook her head. Gloria gave him a look that seemed to say she'd always heard psychiatrists were crazy, and now she believed it.

"Edna, you take Virginia. Gloria, you take Maryland. Let's leave North Carolina till last."

"But, Doctor," Edna protested. "Your phone bill is going to be enormous."

"I'm sure of it," he said. "Now there's one thing we haven't covered. Do you know what it is?"

"Of course," said Edna. "Just how do we get the names of these real-estate companies we're supposed to call?"

"Exactly," he said. "In each state—Annapolis for Maryland, and Richmond for Virginia—there will be a state real-estate commission or board or some such equivalent wording. Start out by calling them, and ask for the names of real-estate agencies—at least two or three for each county on the list. Then you're on your own."

"Holy mackerel," said Gloria.

The morning was almost gone. Returning now to the consulting room, he felt his spirits suddenly sag. Under the idea's spell, while he was outlining it to them, he had realized that it was only the wildest of wild hunches, and doubtless a waste of time and money.

But at least it would not be a waste of *his* time. It was at least an attempt at double-teaming. For, as they moved hesitantly into action, he continued with calls of his own.

He reached Professor Roy Carroway between classes at Columbia.

"Eric Mallory?" said Carroway. "Sure, Dick, I know him. Or rather know of him. I met him once at Princeton. Very bright chap. No, I haven't the faintest idea of what he's doing now. Atomic rockets? Very interesting. Well, I should think by far the most logical spot would be Cape Canaveral."

Cape Canaveral was an impossibility. According to the General, the patient had been moved from his home to Base X by automobile. Even though he could pinpoint Base X only vaguely, he could certainly legitimately estimate that from Florida to a point 250 miles from New York would be a trip of approximately one thousand miles. A good two-day auto trip, and certainly not the ideal means for transporting a demented man wearing a pillowslip. No. He had the feeling that Base X was only a short auto ride from Mallory's home. Just a hunch, but at this point he had to go with his hunches. Time was short.

Through the open doorway he could see Gloria, the receiver to her ear, frowning, reaching down to scratch her leg. Gloria seemed slow and vague, and from the few snatches he overheard he would not give her any accolade for Telephone Personality.

Edna, on the other hand, was a demon. He could hear her dialing, snapping out numbers to the long-distance operator. "Yes, Operator, that is correct. *Yes*. That is *correct*." Edna loved a challenge.

And now Edna was pausing to direct a few words at Gloria. "For the love of Pete," she said with irritation. "You don't have to say 'This is Gloria King calling' every time somebody answers. Then you waste five minutes while they say '*Who?*'

and you say 'Gloria King' and they don't know who Gloria King is from Adam. Give them your name and number toward the end of the conversation when they're ready for it."

"Okay, okay," Gloria said, scratching her leg. "I'll bet when *you* were a teen-ager . . ."

"Oh, don't you give me any of that teen-ager stuff either."

He smiled. The smile faded. He got up and stood at the window, thinking of Mallory as he had looked in the hospital ward. A strange feeling to realize that he alone in the entire nation knew where Mallory was now. His hand hit the window sill. Of course, that's why he'd been followed—the man on the street, the man with the binoculars—while Mallory had been trying to telephone him. Mallory had got away from them. Them? Arbuthnot—Fitzgerald. He must have done the research necessary. Could *he* have been the impersonator? He was a consummate actor. But—

Victor Romagna? Fenton thought of the dirty bills in his safe, of Victor's almost simple-minded attempt to bribe him. But he hadn't asked where Mallory was, he had wanted only to keep Mallory away from his sister. Simple-minded, Fenton thought again, that was the key to Victor, not the stuff of which conspirators and spies are made.

How about Mr. Green?

Mr. Green had left specific phone numbers, specific promises. And though the doctor had turned the originals in, he had kept a record of those letters.

Would it be possible to make a "deal"? To outhoodwink the hoodwinkers?

He headed for the room where the office safe was housed. Passing through, he heard Edna chanting, "Lyons, Peabody and Farnsworth? I have a client interested in buying a certain house which is located in your area . . ."

And Gloria was saying, "Yes, from New York. How are you today? Oh, it's *cold* up here . . . *real* cold."

In the safe he saw Romagna's wad of bills. Behind them was

a small folded slip of paper on which he had written down the three phone numbers.

Returning to the other room, he dialed first the Plaza number. There was no answer.

Next he placed a person-to-person call to Mr. Green at the Plainfield, New Jersey, number.

A child, a girl of perhaps eight or nine, answered.

"Mr. Green, please," the operator said. "Long distance calling."

"Who?"

"Mr. Green, please. Is this the residence of Mr. Green?"

"My daddy is not home," the child said.

"What's your daddy's name?" the doctor asked.

"What is your daddy's name, dear?" the operator repeated.

"My daddy's name is Joseph Stevens."

"Cancel it, please, Operator," he said.

The significance of this penetrated slowly. As a test, he then placed a call to Major Brown at the number Green had given in Annandale, Virginia.

"I'm sorry, Major Brown is not in," a woman said. "He cannot be reached for several days. But if you would like to leave your number . . ."

"No, thanks, Operator," the doctor said. "Cancel it."

TWENTY-THREE

His first reaction was one of fury. A fake, engineered by the General. A matter of extra checks and balances. A way of testing his loyalty—or, to be more exact, of testing his obedience. Testing to see whether he would turn the letters in; whether he would call the numbers. It was small consolation to recall that the letters had stopped coming after he had told of Fitzgerald's visit and had offered to risk the danger. The General had been convinced after that, or perhaps embarrassed.

From the next room, the voices rose and fell in steady feminine counterpoint. The chatter reminded him of something . . .

"How is it going, ladies?" he called.

"It's fun," Gloria trilled.

"Most of them say they'll have to call us back, Doctor," Edna chirped back briskly.

Birds. Yes, there was a curious similarity . . .

He wished that at some time in his life he had taken a course in navigation. Then, like a bird, he could have *sensed* the course of those flights. He wondered if the plane had had a navigator. He thought of the young Negro pilot and of La Guardia.

He called the tower at La Guardia.

The young man who answered was co-operative. He said he would search his records if the doctor would hold on. He returned. The private plane which had left La Guardia at 7:00 p.m. on the day specified was the property of a Mr. Arnold Donahue. Its destination was a private airfield.

"You might call Mr. Donahue, sir."

"Do you know where I might reach him?"

"No, but you might try Washington. I believe he was once a member of Congress."

He tried to place a call. But Washington Information had no listing for a Mr. Arnold Donahue. Like Throckmorton, Mr. Donahue was doubtless an old-time friend of the General.

It was by now eleven-thirty.

"A nice little old town named Bridgewater . . ."

He could still hear Dr. Throckmorton's voice.

He tried.

Information's voice down there was syrupy and sleepy.

"No, Operator, Dr. Throckmorton doesn't have any office here. To tell *you* the truth, I think he's left town. He used to live over at Miss Gibson's house." She gave an early-century-sounding number with three digits.

A woman answered, and said that not only was Throckmorton gone, but that she hoped he wouldn't return.

"Could I talk to the party, Operator? . . . Hello, Miss Gibson, I'm calling from New York. Have you any idea of Dr. Throckmorton's whereabouts?"

"I sure haven't," came the reply. "And far as I'm concerned, I don't care if I never know where that old ski-yunflint is. Stingy nasty old dirty old . . ."

He hung up, thinking that Dr. Throckmorton might be called many things, but certainly not dirty. At least not outwardly. He had a fetish for cleanliness. Maybe old Throckmorton was a lecher.

Dead ends. Hidden like a charm. And a monster at large; not only at large, but protected as though in cotton wool, ready to commit God-knows-what the minute the General took his leave from the Mallory home.

It was just about noon when the storm broke.

One call after another. It was his job to take the incoming calls, while Edna and Gloria pushed on. Voices beguiled him, voices cajoled him, male and female. Houses of all types, houses on creeks and rivers, houses in Virginia, Maryland —were described until his head swam. He heard sweet apologies for a "*painted* drawing room, but it has a wallpapered master bedroom, Chinese décor." Houses with lots of boxwood, but no brick sidewalk. There were "museum pieces." Ante-bellum mansions, houses where George Washington had definitely laid his head, houses which could make his fortune as tearooms, antique shops and exclusive funeral parlors

. . . Prices were quoted, backgrounds of the owners were described—until he couldn't keep the counties or even the states straight. But still no house exactly like Base X.

Lyons, Peabody and Farnsworth? . . . Smith and Smith . . . Mrs. Gussie Croker? . . . A crystal chandelier . . . old boxwood, pier glass . . ." Edna was relentless.

By one the incoming calls were dwindling, and he called a halt. They hadn't found a thing. Beyond this city with its slush and sunshine, in a world of woods and water, lay one old house.

It was undoubtedly a piece of government property.

He sent for sandwiches and coffee. Only Gloria still hung on, her face aglow. Finally, tapped on the shoulder by Edna, she hung up and sighed.

"Gee, what a nice man. His voice is just like Jimmy Stewart's." She sniffled. "It sounds just gorgeous down there too. Do you know what he did? He went duck shooting yesterday . . ."

"Hmm," said Edna. "You ought to be ashamed of yourself. Wasting the doctor's money." She moved to the scribbles on Gloria's desk, read something—turned. "What was that agent's name?"

"Harry," Gloria said. "Harry Moss."

"Did he tell you about this house?"

"Yes, but it's not for sale. It belongs to some old lady."

"Doctor!" Edna exclaimed. "It's got the boxwood, the right wallpaper . . ." She had to decipher the rest of the notes, for they were written in the vaguest penmanship. Edna turned on Gloria. By dint of careful cross-examination it was determined that the rest of the details matched. The house was named Bay View. It had good copper plumbing, and a septic tank. It was in Maryland.

"But it's not for sale," protested Gloria.

Dr. Fenton telephoned Harry Moss.

Mr. Moss was very suave, but Bay View wasn't up for

sale. It *might* be. He'd be happy to inquire. Its owner happened to be in Europe.

"Have you been in this house recently?" the doctor asked.

Mr. Moss frankly hadn't been near the place for years. But he had played there as a boy and knew it well. Its boxwood garden was locally famous, and its wallpaper was original Chinese Chippendale. Did the doctor know that the chandelier had been made in Venice? Its owner was a fancier of harpsichords. The house boasted a secret room and a tunnel underneath the kitchen that was supposed to have been used before the Civil War by runaway slaves. Quite an historical old place, with many legends. It had an orchard, too, and a boathouse. It was really one of the "buys" in the county—if only its owner could ever be persuaded . . .

"Who is its owner?" Dr. Fenton asked.

"An elderly lady. A Miss Ann Donahue."

Donahue!

"Is she related to former Congressman Donahue?" asked Dr. Fenton.

"No. Well, maybe a distant cousin. I couldn't say for sure. Of course we have many other fine old mansions . . ."

"No," Dr. Fenton said. "I think I'll wait for Bay View. I knew it too as a boy. But I've forgotten its exact location. Could you tell me how to get there, please?"

Mr. Moss could and did, in precise detail.

He sent Gloria home feeling well paid and self-important.

When she was gone, he asked Edna if she could stay on through the evening and perhaps until late at night to man the telephone.

She said yes.

"I'm expecting a call from a General Atwood. If it comes through, tell the operator that I have authorized you to accept the call for me and that I left a message for the General."

"All right, sir." Edna said, pencil poised, and throwing him a glance. Her lips twitched. "What is the message, Doctor?"

"This is it." He turned away. But, damn it, she had never betrayed a secret. *Somebody* had to help. Still, it must remain a riddle. " 'The real patient is ill in New York,' " he dictated slowly. " 'There is a double in his place. The wife is in danger. Do not take the patient home.' Right?"

"Right."

"And there's one other thing," he said. "A Dr. Willis at Bellevue Hospital may call about a patient . . ." He went on, still trying to make his voice sound matter-of-fact. The man's name was Mulroy. He was a pneumonia case. She was to keep a record of the reports, and just in case, it might be wise to alert Louisa, too.

But these elaborate final instructions proved unnecessary. Just before he left the office, the call came.

"Dr. Fenton? Dr. Willis calling. Doctor, I'm terribly sorry. Your friend Mr. Mulroy died about ten minutes ago."

TWENTY-FOUR

The country surrounding Bay View was rural, with widely spread-out settlements, and these accessible almost entirely by bus or automobile. To go by train was out of the question. There were no trains that came within a hundred miles of the place. Nor could he reproduce the plane journeys made with Stevens. One commercial airliner sporadically landed in that territory, but weather conditions had canceled all its flights for the past week. As for a private plane, he faced a similar situation. And if by endless telephoning, he managed to find some daring youngster who would fly him down, there was still the problem of the final stage, which must, of necessity, involve a car. Whether there were car-rental agencies in such remote, unurban country, he could not pause at this

163

point to find out. And a taxi, naturally, would be out of the question. The safest and perhaps the fastest bet in the long run would be to drive himself.

Mr. Moss had estimated (no doubt optimistically) that the trip by car could be done with rapid driving in four hours. One took the Jersey Turnpike, crossed the Delaware Bridge, and the roads were decent due south well past a turn-off, which would lead him past a country store. He must watch for this country store very carefully, for after that there was some backing and filling to be done. The entrance to Bay View was heavily wooded, and to be sure he didn't miss it, he must count the miles from the store.

It was almost two-thirty by the time he reached the Jersey side of the Lincoln Tunnel. Already the brightness was going from this winter day. Traffic was heavy. It was as though all the cars and trucks in New York had burst out to make up for the time lost by the snow. Mud splashed against his wheels; horns honked; purple shadows already lay across the Wee-hawken bluffs.

Although the snow still lay deep on the fields on both sides, the turnpike itself had been beautifully cleared. He was over the speed limit more often than under it, and twice, behind him, he heard a siren. But the MD on his license plate gave him immunity, and he did not slow down. Each time the sound of the siren faded.

The countryside, still blanketed with snow, grew beautiful, more rural, with peaceful fields, barns, trees outlined against the dying sun, but he scarcely noticed it, except for anxiety at the rapid sinking of that sun. For long miles he brooded over the strange ordeal, the crucifixion of Eric Mallory.

The sun was gone, the sky a sheet of flame as he crossed the Delaware River. By the time he was well into Maryland, only a flush of red remained. He was in rural open country now, with stubbled corn fields, widely spaced houses. He stopped for gasoline, and while the car was being serviced, telephoned Edna.

The General had not called him.

Twilight, without a moon, lay on the silent landscape. His eyes ached, and with this pause in the momentum, discouragement, a vast sense of futility overcame him. He went into the men's room and dashed some cold water on his face. As he was coming out, he heard far off in the dusk—yes, the sound of a vast cocktail party, the same sound he had heard at the landing field so long ago.

Through it the sounds of laughter rose and fell. He stood transfixed. There were no lights in that direction.

"What's that sound?" he asked. The attendant was checking the oil stick.

"Wild geese, feeding in one of them fields back yonder. Sounds like about a million of 'em, don't it?"

And then, against the dim light that remained in the western sky, he saw a V-formation of them, with their wide wings, their necks like arrows. Once off the ground, they flew in virtual silence, with only an occasional soft honk. But the laughter and the chattering far off continued. Wild geese. He had heard birds, not human beings that first night in October.

He chuckled. Feeling an unreasonable exultation, he got back into the car.

Finally leaving the main highway, he cut back across country, following Mr. Moss's directions to the first turn-off. He was now on the road he had traveled those many nights in the station wagon. But not until he crossed the long bridge did it seem familiar. The bridge had a distinctive rattle. It crossed a body of water called Snapper Creek, a sign said. Soon he passed the country store mentioned by Mr. Moss, the store he had passed many times and never seen. Five and a half miles more, and there would be the right-turn opening to Bay View. He checked his speedometer.

It was difficult not to admire the General for his sure touch.

How wisely he had chosen one of the few unspoiled areas on the East Coast for his particular hideaway. There were no stop lights and no settlements, just woodland, an occasional sagging house lit as though by kerosene lamps, and the store had been so small and insignificant he had almost missed it. It was distinguishable as a store only by a few faded signs plastered over it. SALADA TEA and CLABBER GIRL.

Five and a half miles . . . Mr. Moss must have miscalculated, or forgotten. For at five and a half miles exactly, cypress trees rose up impenetrably, and when he got out of the car to walk, his feet sank into a swamp. Water, shining and black, stretched just beyond. Five and a half miles was wrong.

Slowly now, inching forward, making U-turns, and retracing his way back and forth on the desolate road, without even the moon to help, he sought the entrance.

It *had* to be on the right. The station wagon had always turned right. And through pine woods. Yet pine woods were everywhere. Wouldn't a house of the importance and distinction of Bay View even be marked? If so, of course, they would have removed the sign. At least a good mile past the spot Mr. Moss had indicated he saw an opening, barely wide enough for one car, leading into the silent gloom of a forest. He nosed the car in, and moved forward over a deeply rutted road. The trees closed in around him, and he heard their branches brush the roof of the car.

It seemed a much longer road than he remembered, but he was taking it more slowly than the driver of that station wagon ever had. The high beam of his headlights picked out stumps, the eyes of animals. He was getting close now. Taking a flashlight from the glove compartment, he got out.

Even the smells were familiar, and the softness of the earth. When he came to the small bluff, felt the wet pine needles beneath his feet, and then the gravel, when he saw the footbridge, there was no longer any doubt.

He could close his eyes (which for a second he did) and *know*, more by the feel of his feet than the reality, that it was

Base X. The reality before his eyes was more confusing. It was different in many respects from what he had imagined. He had never known how these woods curved round that offshore island, like the pincers of a crab. Or that a rowboat lay half in water, half on the beach, complete with crab net and pail. Or that the footbridge crossed a swamp. He had always imagined that it crossed deep water, remembering Stevens' concern. And the house actually wasn't on an island, but on a spit of land, with swampland intervening. It did face open water. It had a boathouse. Where were the sentries? There had always been one on duty at the picket gate, and now that he thought about it, it seemed strange they had not seen his headlights approaching.

He crossed the bridge.

It had the loose boards he remembered. Still unaccosted, he crossed the lawn, an unmowed, spongy stubble. The house loomed dark and silent behind its aisle of giant boxwood. There was the picket gate. It was a handsome frame house, three-story, large, of colonial design. He thought about that tunnel and that "secret" room. He opened the gate. Its clatter was familiar. Here was the old brick sidewalk and that pungent smell.

The darkness of the place of course was—habitual. No lights would ever show through those boards. But—though the boxwood brushed his sleeves, and the protruding brick was where it should be, and the porch echoed with the proper hollowness—he knew that Base X was no more.

He could tell for certain by its windows.

All the boards had been removed. Draperies had been hung. He trained his flashlight, peering in at furniture utterly unfamiliar.

Gone was the leather couch which should be near this window. In its place was—a harpsichord. A handsome rug stretched off into deep shadow. He could see tables, lamps and portraits. No sign of a desk, a gooseneck lamp. He turned the flashlight higher, stooped down and craned his neck for sight of the chandelier. It was there, and the wallpaper looked like the familiar red and gold.

But they had restored the house's interior grandeur so that even Miss Ann Donahue might never know what had happened here.

Stupid to stand here, admiring their efficiency. The fact was —that he had come for nothing.

When had they left?

The trash might give an indication, the date on a newspaper perhaps. But on the other hand they couldn't have left before today. *Why not?* Four days of silence had gone by. Still he clung with desperation to Angela's and Victor's words: "Saturday. They're bringing him home on Saturday." He hurried to the back of the house. It had a neat back porch, but no cans, not a scrap of paper, not a broken egg nor coffee grounds upon the well-swept ground. But would they leave their trash in cans for a possible prowler to examine? Behind the house there was underbrush, some apple trees. Tramping through them, he caught the odor of charred wood.

Yes, here was the trash pit. Here they'd burned the evidence. Nothing left but ash. But the *ash was warm.*

He ran back to the footbridge.

If they had left by car, there would be tire marks. He found only old ruts and the fresh marks of his own tires.

They had not left by car.

Through the "tunnel used by runaway slaves"? It seemed ridiculous. An old, probably caved-in mess, that after all might just be legendary. This was swampy land. But how else?

The water here was very low. Near the bank he could see the bottom. It did not look as though a boat of any size could land here. But—there *was* a boathouse.

He had ignored it before. Till tonight he had not even known of its existence. But it was perhaps by boat that they had moved Eric Mallory's diabolical double. He made his way gingerly to the end of the small dock. It seemed rotten. The water here was so shallow he could see a tin can at the bottom.

168

And then, as he moved the beam of the flashlight, he saw a piece of colored paper floating close to one of the pilings.

It was a Baby Ruth wrapper.

He stopped, fished it out. Its color was still bright, unfaded. And the odor of chocolate and peanuts still clung to it. Why, old sweet-tooth Stevens had probably not even picked the fragments from his molars yet.

He flashed his light on a piling. The level of the water was now a good two and a half feet below the top of the wet mark on the piling. The tide was way down. At high tide there must have been at least three feet of water at the end of the dock. Plenty of fair-sized launches had less draft than that.

How long had it been since high tide?

And where did this creek lead?

TWENTY-FIVE

Hurrying back to the car, he spread the map on the front seat and trained the flashlight on it.

Snapper Creek was marked in minute lettering. It twisted crookedly to a river, and this river to a larger river, and this in turn to the Chesapeake.

"If they went by boat . . ." he said aloud.

To judge from the size of the lettering, the towns in the immediate area were all very small, no more than villages and hamlets. There was no town that sounded as if it might be a government reservation.

Above the restless wind in the pines, he heard the steady drone of a plane.

"But hell," he said aloud. "The people around here would know."

They would surely know. They might not know that it

was a place where atomic research was carried on. But at least they would know that it was a government base of some kind. He studied the map again. A government base would have U.S. marked in parentheses beneath its name, or Fed. Gov't., or some such marking.

Pushing the map aside, he started the car and backed it close to the stand of pine. Through the windshield he could see the lights of the plane. He paused. It was circling, preparing to land perhaps at the very landing field which he and Stevens had used. But as he watched, it began climbing again.

He finished turning around and jolted back out through the woods to the highway, where he turned left, heading back to the country store.

Just a few hundred yards down the road he saw a car backing out of one of the entrance lanes that he had tried on his way to Bay View.

"How do?"

"Good evening."

A woman in an apron stood behind the counter. An old man in a red-plaid hunting cap sat in a rocker next to a wood stove. The store was very warm. It smelled of cheese and sausage. A brace of duck hung from a beam.

"Gas?" the woman asked, wiping her hands on her apron and heading for the door.

"No. No, thanks. I wonder if you'd be good enough to tell me—is there a government base or installation of some kind around here?"

"Tucker Point," the woman said in a singsong.

"Yep, Tucker Point," the old man said. "About ten mile." They looked at him curiously.

"Is that the way it's listed in the phone book?" The doctor asked, heading for the door. There was a telephone booth outside.

"Well . . ." the man said. "You just look under U.S. Government. Helen, you know their number? I can't rightly call it to mind. But you just look under the U.S. Government, and there it is—Tucker Point."

"Thanks," the doctor said.

There it was indeed. He placed the call quickly.

"Tucker Point."

The switchboard operator's voice was crisp. No trace of the dialect he had just heard in the store.

"Dr. Eric Mallory's residence, please."

She rang and went off the line. Presently she returned, and said, "I'll ring again," and again closed the key. He waited. "I'm sorry, sir. That line does not answer."

"All right then, Operator. May I speak to General Atwood, please?"

"I'll give you Information," she said.

Information said there was no listing for General Atwood. "Then will you let me have the officer of the day, please? This is an emergency."

Information flashed the operator. "Connect with OD, please."

Another buzz. A woman answered. "Corporal Wildman."

"Officer of the day, please. An emergency call."

"Captain Howe has just stepped out for a moment. Could I help you?"

"Yes." And he was shouting now. "You'll have to. Do you have any way of getting word to General Atwood?"

She hesitated. "I don't believe I know of a General Atwood, sir."

"All right then, damn it," he said wildly. "Please get word to *somebody* in authority. *Dr. Eric Mallory is dead.* Do you have that? Dr. Eric Mallory is dead. A double is taking his place. Mrs. Mallory's life is in danger."

"Who is this calling, please?"

"My name is Fenton. Dr. Richard Fenton. General Atwood knows me well. I was Dr. Mallory's psychiatrist. Fenton. *Fenton.*"

"Thank you, Dr. Fenton. I will report your call."

"Report my *call*. Listen, this is an *emergency!*"

"Yes, sir. I will be glad to report the information you have given me, sir."

"Oh, my God!" he groaned. There seemed to be something deliberately evasive in her manner. "Listen, please. Can you tell me this then? Do you know whether Dr. Mallory or the man supposed to be Dr. Mallory was brought home today?"

"Not to my knowledge, sir. Dr. Mallory was scheduled to arrive today, but there was a delay." In the background there was the sound of another phone. Short, staccato, insistent rings. "Thank you, sir."

And she hung up.

He jammed the receiver down on the hook and went back into the store.

"Find it all right, did you?" the old man asked.

"Yes," he said. "Thanks. I wonder if you could tell me how to get to Tucker Point, please."

"You can't go in unless you got business there," the old man said.

"Maybe he's *got* business there," the woman said, looking at him curiously.

"Well, of course, if you've got business there, that's different," the man said. "It's only about ten mile. It used to be old man Horton's tract and he sold it to the guvmunt for near about a hundred thousand dollars. Wasn't it a hundred thousand dollars, Helen? Used to be the best rock fishing in the county right off that point. Now you take a rowboat and you can't get within two miles of it. By water, I mean. And then, of course, the whole place is got barb wire all around it and a senchary gate and I don't know what all it ain't got."

"Can you tell me how to get there?" the doctor asked.

"Sure, you can't hardly miss it. You go down about a mile and you come to a little place called Maple and you turn left and follow right on in . . . Had quite a time out there this morning. Fellow committed suicide."

"Is that so?" The doctor turned from the door. "Who was it, do you know?"

"No, but some say he was a doctor of medicine."

"Was his name Throckmorton?" the doctor asked sharply.

"I don't rightly know," the old man said. "I never did hear his name called, did you, Helen? But he shot hisself clean through the head, according to one of the soldiers stops here for gas."

For a moment longer, the doctor stood there, frowning. Then, thanking them, he closed the door.

As he walked to the car, the sound of his feet crunching over the graveled drive was very loud in the deep country stillness. He smelled the odor of swamp water. Another branch of Snapper Creek? By water, Base X was close . . .

TWENTY-SIX

He slumped wearily behind the wheel in the deep quiet, unable for a moment to summon the energy to start the car. What lay ahead? Another wild goose chase? It had been a long hard day. Since 4:00 A.M. he had not let down once. And maybe the entire trip down here was a fiasco.

He had found Base X, had gotten through to Tucker Point. He had delivered his message to Garcia in the person of a WAC corporal. And it had been received with nonchalance.

The fake Mallory had not been taken home. There was strong reason to believe that Throckmorton had killed himself. What else could it all add up to but that the General knew? That the General had taken the double off somewhere, perhaps to Washington, for detention . . . and that the surveillance networks were combing the East Coast for the real Eric Mallory.

They had access to police tickers.

And Angela? If the General had spared her the news, which it seemed he would do for the time being, then Angela perhaps had gone off for the evening, perhaps to nothing more momentous than a movie . . .

He felt abruptly very old and rather foolish.

He had failed to cure the real Mallory. He had failed to detect the presence of the double. And in New York he had been always one step behind, when, to have hospitalized Mallory sooner, might have meant saving his life.

Shakily he lit a cigarette. It was the last one in his pack.

But, damn it, Mallory was dead. And—it was the decent thing to help her all he could. She had a right to know about her husband's final hours. She would have to plan the burial arrangements. He grunted, remembering that even this he should probably not tell her until he had cleared it with the General.

Well, red tape be damned. He would go to Tucker Point and wait for her. He was here. What would a few more hours matter? He would go there, even though it might mean waiting for her outside a barbed-wire fence.

Returning to the telephone booth, he put through a call to Edna. No one had called. He told her to close up and go home.

Crossing the gravel to his car again, he took out his key case and fumbled for the ignition key, then froze, listening intently.

A scream had come from the direction of the swamp.

Faint, far off, but from the spot he'd earmarked as Base X. Sound traveled far over water. A scream. It was not a bird. In the wintry silence it came again. A *woman's* scream. Another. Straight across that creek.

Listening, he recalled the car which he had passed—and the circling plane above the woods. He started the engine with a roar, lurched out into the highway.

He left the car on the main road and made his way down the dark entrance lane on foot. He heard no more screams.

There were only the sounds of his own stumbling, his own heavy breathing. Branches slapped against his face, he slipped in mud, tripped over stumps. He dared not keep the flashlight on more than a second.

Emerging finally from the stygian aisle, he saw the car parked in the clearing. It was a Buick, a light-colored Buick —the same car, he now felt sure, which he had seen a while ago on his way over to the store. Mallory had owned a light blue Buick.

He approached it cautiously. It was empty. On the front seat lay a violet scarf.

Why? What had possessed her . . . ?

Furtively he slipped down the bluff. Across the swamp the old house loomed as dark and silent as it had been an hour before, but in its very silence there was something ominous.

He hurried across the bridge. And then, crossing the lawn that led to the gate, he saw the plane.

A *seaplane*, for God's sake!

Taking cover behind the gate under the boxwood's giant foliage, he looked at it again. The plane was moored near the end of the dock. Its running lights were turned out. It resembled a huge, ungainly insect, bobbing gently beyond the tumble-down silhouette of the boathouse.

And still, the enormous silence. He crouched there among the boxwood, waiting for the sound of his own breathing to subside, for his heart to quiet.

For no good reason that he could fathom, he kept thinking of Louisa's birthday party, of the elderly lady in blue lace who was concerned about orphans. And then he saw himself standing before a judge, signing papers that would permit him to adopt young Johnny Mallory, who, in the span of one day's swift events, could by now conceivably be an orphan himself.

They, the bastards, must have come here for that double. The plan must have been that he would be taken home, then he would persuade or force Angela Mallory to drive him back here. Very smart. Since Base X would be deserted by then, and it was only ten miles from Tucker Point. If there was trouble, Angela would be a shield. A hostage for further bargaining. Nice guys!

But if the General had *not* taken the double home, how had they gotten her?

He sidled through the boxwood, startled to hear the noise its prickly branches made. And then, as he neared the foot of the porch steps, he heard voices.

Indistinguishable. A low formless hum, but voices unmistakably. They seemed to be coming from the front room, that room where for so many weeks he had talked to Eric Mallory and then to a man who was not Eric Mallory.

He ducked beneath the porch. A smell of damp earth and decaying wood enveloped him. He crawled and squirmed his way over the soft, evil-smelling earth and pressed his ear to the ancient brick foundation. The voices were filtering down through the old floor boards, low, sometimes fading, but he who had had long practice before a canvas screen, began to catch the drift.

A man's voice, vaguely familiar.

"Oh, but, Mrs. Mallory, *baby, really* . . ." Something that sounded like a chuckle. "You must appreciate that we've invested quite a chunk of time and money in this . . . enterprise."

It was Fitzgerald, or Arbuthnot, whatever his name might be, sounding just as suave, just as smooth as on the day he had entered the doctor's office and posed as Mallory's college roommate.

He lost the next few sentences. The suave voice was still speaking. Something scuttled past his shoulder blade, rustled for a second or two, and he caught only "a lady pays for being married to a genius. For being married, let's say, to a valuable piece of merchandise. Honey, don't you know there's a *war* on?"

"Come awn, come awn!" a deep voice growled.

"So please, please tell us where your husband is, Mrs. Mallory," said the smooth voice.

"I've told you." There. At last. It was Angela. "He is with the General. He was supposed to come home today, but he didn't. I thought he was out here. Dr. Fenton called . . ."

Dr. Fenton. Down in the darkness his cheeks burned. So—the bastards must have faked his voice. Poor kid. But at least she was alive. Her voice was thin, pitched unnaturally high, obviously frightened. But she wasn't sobbing.

"Your *real* husband, your *real* husband," the deep voice snarled.

"My *real* husband?"

"Now look, honey lamb—" the smooth one now was burlesquing a southern accent. "Looks to me like we're gonna have to take you for a little spin in our little ole seaplane, you know what I mean?"

Its very lightness was enough to chill the blood.

Richard Fenton felt a surge of blind hatred, of insane rage. He, who had dedicated his life to eradicating hatred and violence from the nature of human beings, was crawling and squirming his way out from under the porch, bent on murder.

But by the time he had reached the sidewalk, the frenzied impulse had abated, giving way to common sense. He was forty-two years old, unarmed, a man who in recent years had taken no more violent exercise than moving from a desk to a consulting couch.

If he had anything to give, it was the ability to think. Not hard bone and muscle.

For a few seconds he crouched there, looking from house to plane to bridge, his mind playing over the possibilities as it might over a series of chess moves.

As in the case of the real-estate hunch, the idea was better than none at all. And it was better than running back to his car, and driving ten miles more to a sentry gate. In times of crisis, it was necessary to act almost from instinct. And his instinct was not only to save Angela, but to do those monsters in.

Perhaps this was his day for hunches.

And perhaps, on the other hand, his luck had run out. He would know very shortly.

He ran as rapidly and as silently as possible now, out the gate, across the lawn and across the footbridge. The rowboat he had noticed had not been moved. The pail and the crab net were still in it, along with one oar.

He lifted out the pail and approached the pale blue Buick.

Siphoning, of course, was out of the question. But a sharp stick might do it.

Or better still . . .

Deliberately, his back to Base X, he searched the glove compartment. He found a screw driver, a pair of pliers and a road map. The lane beyond was impenetrable; he could see nothing for the surrounding trees. But he must concentrate on what he now must do. It would take time and skill. He could only count on Fitzgerald's garrulousness . . .

Stuffing the road map in his pocket, he lifted the Buick hood and with the pliers began to jerk out spark plugs, all of them. These he tossed behind him into the woods. It would not pay to leave them *anything*.

This done, he slid beneath the car.

Lying on his back, he drove the screw driver hard into the under side of the gasoline tank. End of Buick. The gasoline began to spurt. Reaching back for the bucket, he slid it under the jet of gasoline, forcing himself to wait until it was just short of full.

He let the rest dribble on the pine needles. Carrying the bucket, he went down the bluff. Still no sign of figures crossing the lawn. He began to grope along the beach for driftwood. He pried loose a rock about the size of a potato.

These bits of Maryland he wrapped up in the road map,

until he had a package, ready for mailing. He trussed the package securely with his necktie.

Now—this was something like it.

Moving with almost stoic calm, he set the bucket of gasoline in the boat and dropped the package carefully beside it. Shoving the boat off, wading after it, he stepped cautiously in and picked up the single oar.

Now poling, now paddling, trying not to look at the house or even think what could be happening, he gradually shortened the distance between the shoreline and the plane. Dark water gurgled and flowed beneath. Water also gurgled about his shoes. The damned boat must have a leak. When he moved, the bucket swayed precariously. Some of the gasoline slopped out. He picked the package up, examined it.

But, thank God, this rowboat had one bit of necessary equipment. A rope hung from its bow. The rowboat bumped against a pontoon. Bobbing away, he caught the mooring line. And having knotted the two ropes, all he had to do was climb from a shifty rowboat to pontoon, then to cabin door, at the same time guarding the bucket and the package.

It would be plenty cold in that creek. And it was plenty deep out here. There would be no Johannssen to fish him out.

The memory of Mallory's ordeal spurred on his efforts. Carefully, hampered by his overcoat, he placed the bucket up on the pontoon. Then, managing to hold it steady, he dragged himself from bobbing boat to plane, holding the boat to the last second with one ankle.

The cabin door was unlocked.

He worked rapidly, feverishly now. The job was almost pleasurable. He poured the gasoline along the floor, over the two bucket seats, leaving an inch of fluid in the bucket.

In another moment he was back again in the boat. He heaved a sigh of satisfaction.

Now it was only a question of casting off the line, maneuvering the boat into position, saturating the package with the remaining gasoline, and lighting a few matches. Not quite. He

179

stood at the bow at last in a direct line with the cabin door, and took careful aim. The paper sizzled, became a flaming torch. He threw it—straight for the cabin door, and said a prayer.

It was a perfect hit.

Then he poled like hell.

To his amazement, nothing occurred. When he reached the shelter of the boxwood again, the damned thing was still out there, rocking quietly—dark as pitch. No. To his intense relief, he began to see a lurid glow from inside the cabin. Tongues of flame licked out. In another moment . . .

An eye for an eye. Fire in return for fire. Fire had been their trump card when they kidnapped Mallory.

One short, very soft explosion. He faced the front door. How many of them were there? How much time would he really have? He had been toying with a fantastic notion—run into the house as soon as they came out, catch her by the hand, and somehow find that marvelous "tunnel underneath the kitchen." But his mind made mincemeat of it now. The tunnel might be a myth. The General had not used it. If it were ever open, Security would have known about it and blocked it off.

Another explosion roared behind him. Deafening. He could hear the flames. Acrid smoke and burning gasoline. The door burst open. Three men came running down the sidewalk.

Their curses made him smile.

All of them. Three was all. She was in the dark and musty hallway. Hands tied. Something about her mouth.

"Angela . . ."

He had no flashlight any more. He could only feel her terror. But light from the fire outside began to fill the rooms. He unloosed her bonds, he murmured reassurance.

Taking her hand, he dragged her forward down the steps, out through the boxwood. But there was a man now at the picket gate. There were angry shouts from the front lawn. They could never risk that bridge.

180

Run back into the house? Try to find that "secret" room? They might never find it. They would be trapped.

They must go as Mallory had gone . . . through water, *his* last resort. But this was creek water, not the ocean. Base X was not an island. That footbridge crossed a swamp. And the woods curved round this swamp like a crab's pincers. If they had to swim a little, well, okay. He took her round the house, keeping to the garden, avoiding the boathouse side. Beyond the apple trees he slid down the soft bank.

Hand in hand. They floundered through the swamp, scrambled up the opposite bank, and raced into the woods.

As they reached his car, three cars came speeding down the highway. Nearing the entrance to Base X, they slowed with a screeching of brakes.

"The cavalry," Dr. Fenton muttered.

A brilliant spotlight on the lead car shone full in his face.

"Fenton!" an amazed voice called. "That isn't you?"

"Yes, sir," the doctor said. "It's just old me and Angela Mallory, General Atwood."

"Amazing," said the General.

"I think," said Dr. Fenton, "you'll find the chaps you're looking for back there in the bushes."

TWENTY-SEVEN

Angela Mallory sat in a blue wing chair, a military topcoat wrapped around her. A fire had been lit in the marble fireplace. Its light played over her long loose hair and her sad pale face. Tears glistened in the beautiful eyes.

The General paced to the far end of the room. He returned, stood next to her chair and put a hand on her shoulder. "I

181

feel personally responsible for your husband's death, Mrs. Mallory," he said in a low voice.

Dr. Fenton watched her expression. She sat immobile, eyes upon the fire, tears unheeded. "Please don't feel that way, General," she said. "I don't hold anyone to blame. I . . ."

She paused, looking down at the hearth.

The General waited respectfully, but she did not go on.

"Even so, I do feel responsible," the General said finally. "And I feel that I should explain to you where we made our mistake."

He had already told Dr. Fenton where the miscalculation had been made, and now he was repeating it for her in low tones of humility, even of disbelief, as though he were still trying to reason it out for himself.

The mistake lay in a belief held by the hierarchy of Counterespionage that the dangerous elements were known agents of Iron Curtain countries. The movements of all known agents had been under constant surveillance throughout the affair at Base X. The movements of all known agents had been accounted for at all times.

The band of men responsible for the kidnapping of Eric Mallory had not been foreign agents at all, at least not in the usual sense. They were, instead, simply a group of thugs with experience in smuggling and peddling of dope, and newly engaged, beginning with Mallory, in trafficking in human beings who might bring a price.

Eric Mallory was to have been sold to Red China for one million dollars. His job—to chart a pathway past the moon.

"And of course another mistake," the General went on, "was something I never dreamed could be a mistake. To think, even to suspect that old Bill Throckmorton . . ." He paused. "Bill should have married," he said abruptly.

Angela did not stir.

"And we very nearly completed the botch," the General said, "by losing you, Mrs. Mallory."

"It would have been my own fault," Angela murmured.

And in a way it had been. She was a simple woman.

His dogmatism gradually shaken by Dr. Fenton's strong doubt of the cure, the General had finally been shocked into an awareness of the double's existence with the discovery of Throckmorton's suicide that morning. Accompanied by Stevens and a couple of strong-armed agents, he had holed up with the double (an ex-actor who had forsworn the theater for heroin) in a country hotel near Tucker Point.

From the timetable touched upon by the General, Dr. Fenton figured that the confession finally was obtained at just about the same minute that he was setting out in the rowboat with his bucket of gasoline. The General had moved swiftly after that. The capture of "Fitzgerald" and his two thugs had been rather ridiculously easy. With the hood up, all three had been bent over the motor of Angela's car, trying to get it started. When they saw the lights approaching, they ran, but were caught after a short chase through the woods.

Angela had begun receiving telephone calls at four o'clock today, asking for Mallory. When it became apparent to the conspirators that something had slipped up, they had changed their tune. At nine o'clock, a man who said he was Dr. Fenton, and who sounded exactly like him, had told her to come to Bay View and "help with therapy." There had been a "crisis." Her husband needed her.

She had not hesitated.

"General . . ." Stevens was at the doorway. "Could we see you a second, please?"

The captive trio was in the kitchen, about to be removed from the premises.

"Excuse me a second, please." The General started for the door, then turned. "By the way, Doctor, it's about time I asked *you* a question. It just occurred to me. How did you ever find this place? Did your blindfold slip one night?"

"No, sir." The doctor told of the calls to the real-estate agents.

183

The General smiled. "Pretty good. Pretty damned good." He left the room.

Angela still stared into the fire. Muddy, in stained trousers damp with creek water and gasoline, the doctor stood beside the harpsichord. "You can be very proud of your husband, Mrs. Mallory," he said at last. "He left his country a tremendous legacy of genius. He jumped into an icy river rather than serve a foreign power. He jumped, in effect, to his death."

She spoke in a strained, small voice. It was as though she had not been listening to what he had said. "Eric was a very strange man. A very good man . . ." She leaned back. "But not really of this earth." Abruptly she turned, her dark eyes wet. "Who—really killed him?" she asked.

And it was strange that at the same moment the same question had run through his own mind.

Who, or what, had really killed Eric Mallory?

One had to begin with his breakdown. And the breakdown? It could only be assumed, but it was believable enough, that Mallory, doubtless at Wichita Falls to begin with, had been approached and an offer made. When he refused, there had been threats on his life, and on the life of his wife and child. The crackup had followed.

But one must begin, of course, much further back than Wichita Falls.

The doctor looked toward the archway, just an arch again, leading into a shadowy dining room. But in his mind's eye he saw a desk, a microphone and a huge canvas screen.

They had come so close that night before the fire. And if there had been another night, he thought. If I could have spent just one more decent session with him, perhaps . . . just a few more hours—then the mystery, like a black silk kerchief, might have fallen from the soul of Eric Mallory.

". . . come back . . . next time . . ." He seemed to hear the voice pleading.

But there had been no next time.

"*Who?*" she asked again. And her face was twisted now with deep grief.

"I don't know, Mrs. Mallory," the doctor said. "That's something we will probably never answer."

The room was very still. A gray log crumbled apart. Presently the General opened the door. "We just bundled off the Rover Boys," he said. "Your clothes are dry now, Mrs. Mallory." He was carrying the doctor's shoes.

He set the room to rights while Angela changed upstairs. Finally, with a rueful look, he switched off the crystal chandelier. "This old house didn't exactly bring us luck, did it?"

Clasping the doctor on the shoulder, as Angela, pale and composed, came down into the hallway, he told them to go on ahead. "I'll catch up with you. I want to be sure there isn't any danger of . . ."

He didn't finish. Had he been about to say "of fire"?

The old clock ticking in the hallway began to chime the hour of twelve.

They stepped into the pure, fresh air.

Crossing the lawn, Angela paused. She looked up at the sky and shivered. The doctor followed her gaze. The stars had broken through the haze. The night was crystal clear. The Milky Way was bright. Stars, by the millions and trillions . . .

He took her arm and helped her across the bridge.

LUCILLE FLETCHER is famous, of course, for her unforgettable *Sorry, Wrong Number*, originally a radio show, later a novel, and finally a motion picture for which she herself wrote the screen play. She has also written many syndicated short shorts and countless scripts for Suspense and Orson Welles' shows.

She was born in Brooklyn, educated in public schools there, and took a B.A. degree at Vassar. She is married and lives in Arlington, Virginia, with her husband and her two daughters. "My hobbies," she says, "are playing the piano and writing, although the major part of my life is spent in housekeeping and cooking meals."

had been a major scientist. It was important that he continue to be. He had gone off the rails; he had blown his top. When he talked rationally, he talked treason. The General said to Dr. Fenton, "You may very well be our final hope."

Fenton was a distinguished and brilliant doctor. He knew it was an impossible assignment—how could you get at a man whom you couldn't even see? about whom you were told nothing but stark statistics?—but he consented. Patriotism? Medical dedication? Or was it that the General had said, "If you take this on, you will be in some personal danger"?

From his first moment on the plane, Dr. Fenton began to assemble clues to where the patient was hidden. He wore a blindfold, but he could count the seconds of the flight. He was led, stumbling, out of the plane, but the scent of honeysuckle was inescapable, and there was an identifiable texture to the ground on which he walked. These observations he made instinctively—he had been trained to observe with all his senses—and they became matters of life and death when, weeks later, seemingly, the case was finished. Successfully finished.

Because Dr. Fenton knew it wasn't